Scary Urban Legends

Tom Baker

Illustrations by John Eng

Schiffer Publishing Ltd®

4880 Lower Valley Road, Atglen, Pennsylvania 19310

Ouija is a registered trademark of Parkers Brothers.

Schiffer Books are available at special discounts for bulk purchases for sales promotions or premiums. Special editions, including personalized covers, corporate imprints, and excerpts can be created in large quantities for special needs. For more information contact the publisher:

Published by Schiffer Publishing Ltd.
4880 Lower Valley Road
Atglen, PA 19310
Phone: (610) 593-1777; Fax: (610) 593-2002
E-mail: Info@schifferbooks.com

For the largest selection of fine reference books on this and related subjects, please visit our web site at

www.schifferbooks.com

We are always looking for people to write books on new and related subjects. If you have an idea for a book please contact us at the above address.

This book may be purchased from the publisher. Include $5.00 for shipping. Please try your bookstore first. You may write for a free catalog.

In Europe, Schiffer books are distributed by
Bushwood Books
6 Marksbury Ave.
Kew Gardens
Surrey TW9 4JF England
Phone: 44 (0) 20 8392-8585; Fax: 44 (0) 20 8392-9876
E-mail: info@bushwoodbooks.co.uk
Website: www.bushwoodbooks.co.uk

Copyright © 2010 by Tom Baker
Library of Congress Control Number: 2010928876
All illustrations courtesy of John Eng
Text courtesy of Benjamin Thomas Baker

Designed by Stephanie Daugherty
Type set in Batik Regular/New Baskerville BT/Humanst521 BT
ISBN: 978-0-7643-3587-7
Printed in The United States of America

Contents

Dedication

This book is dedicated to
Erika and Kara and Britain and
Caleb and Christopher.
(For when they are older.)

Also, to my Aunt Terri,
my mother Brenda Durham,
and my entire family
for their love and support.

Acknowledgments

Special acknowledgements go to Dinah Roseberry, John Eng, Mary Leffler and the staff of the Marion Public Library, the staff of the Waldenbooks at Five Points Mall in Marion, Indiana, Marla Brooks from Para-X Radio, The hosts of the Indianapolis Ghost Hunters radio show, and Rev. Steve Colter. As to anyone else I've left out, my deepest apologies, because you, too, I am grateful. It wasn't intentional.

Foreword

If you like scary stories (and most everyone does), then you're going to love reading this book! It's a collection of scary tales based on "urban legends," or as the excellent website Snopes (www.snopes.com) explains:

> Urban legends are a specific class of legend, differentiated from "ordinary" legends by their being provided and believed as accounts of actual incidents that befell or were witnessed by someone the teller almost knows (e.g., his sister's hairdresser's mechanic). These tales are told as true, local, and recent occurrences, and often contain names of places or entities located within the teller's neighborhood or surrounding region.

In other words, urban legends are stories that people believe to be true, and they play on our fears and concerns and serve to warn us of things we should and shouldn't do. Some urban legends are sad, some are funny, and some are just downright… scary. The stories told in this volume are all scary urban legends, because those are, often, the most fun and dramatic of all.

Nearly all of the stories in this volume are false (probably…), based on nothing more than rumors passed around by people who believe them to be true. However, two of the stories in this book ARE based on real events. We'll leave you to guess as you read which ones they are, and give you the answer at the end of the book.

So sit back, get comfortable, and be prepared to be scared. We're going on a little trip through twenty odd tales of weird and wild happenings. But which stories are true, and which are only terror tales? You will have to decide. Is it true that I'm wrong and they ALL are true? Could that be possible? Some think so… could so many be that wrong? Sure they can. Well, maybe.

Buckle up!

The Hook

Janet and Brad were necking in the car. It was a dark, lonely night, and the two kids had pulled into the local "lover's lane" so they could share a romantic evening. It was a little chilly, so Brad put his arm around Janet to warm her up a little.

"Oh Brad, let's get some music on the radio! It's too quiet out here. It's giving me the creeps."

"Sure thing, babe!" said Brad, twiddling the dial on the radio. He got a bunch of static at first (the reception out here was terrible, for some strange reason), but suddenly, a very good rock and roll song burst forth through all the static. It sounded like jarring punk rock, and Brad liked it quite a bit, but Janet said, "No! That's not going to do it at all! Find something...romantic."

He frowned, twiddled the knob again, and finally hit on a station that was playing something that sounded like elevator music.

"There, that's a lot better!" Janet sounded a little more relaxed now, and sat back, letting Brad put his arm around her and draw her close. She was really starting to warm up to him, and Brad felt like the evening might just turn out all right after all. He leaned over to try and steal a kiss, when suddenly, an announcement broke in over the radio:

"We regret to interrupt this program, but we've just received word from Farmington Asylum for the Criminally Insane that a dangerous mental patient, known only to staff at the asylum as 'The Hook,' because of the hook he wears in place of his missing hand, has reportedly escaped from the asylum and is believed to be heading north, toward Wilmington. The man, whose true identity has been a mystery for years, but who is believed to have killed many innocent people and is considered extremely dangerous, was last spotted by witnesses running through the woods surrounding the institution, before disappearing to avoid capture. As startling and frightening as this is to report, ladies and gentleman, we must urge all of the listeners in our area to be on the lookout and to exercise extreme caution if they encounter this maniac. He is to be considered extremely dangerous. He also, reportedly, seeks out many of his victims among teenagers who park in lonely, isolated spots, or 'lover's lanes' as they are called…"

"Oh, Brad, maybe we should be going! I don't like the thought of being out here all alone, with that maniac on the loose!" Janet looked, all of a sudden, like she was going to come unglued.

Brad laughed, and then switched the radio off. He leaned over, gave Janet a kiss on the cheek and said, "Relax, babe! That nutcase is probably miles away from here by now. He wouldn't dare stick around, what with everybody looking for him and everything. He may be crazy, but I bet he's not stupid."

Janet crossed her arms over her chest, looking as if she was going to start pouting (which really annoyed him), but she slowly seemed to come around to his reassurances. She loosened up a little, and soon they were holding each other close, kissing passionately.

"Hey, what was that?" Janet suddenly pulled away from him, with a nervous look on her face.

"It was nothing," said Brad, who wanted to keep kissing. "Just the wind rattling some branches against the car, is all."

"No, I heard something out there. It sounded like a few footsteps, and then something scraping…Oh, Brad, I'm scared! I want to go home! I want you to take me home right now!"

"Janet, I swear, there's nothing wrong! There's nobody out there! You want me to go take a look?"

"No!" screamed Janet. "Don't you dare leave me alone in this car! Brad, if you love me at all, you'll drive us both out of here and take me home right this instant!"

"Janet..." Brad tried to reason with her (he was already missing all the hot kisses), but he could tell she was ready to throw a fit, so with a heavy sigh he pulled away, turned the key in the ignition, pumped the gas, and said, "I think this is crazy. That hooked maniac is probably in another state by now, and you want to go home and cower under the covers."

"Better safe than sorry," said Janet with a little pout on her lips.

So he revved up the convertible, backed out of the old wooded cul-de-sac, sending up dirt and gravel flying in all directions, and headed back down the lonely country lane toward home.

He pulled up in front of Janet's house, which was big and bright and in a good neighborhood. He knew that, right now, her mom and dad would be waiting for her, nervously, in front of the television, carefully sipping tea or coffee, and watching the clock.

He got out to open the door for her. (Have to look good in front of the parents; after all, they would certainly be watching him through the blinds.)

Suddenly, as he walked behind the convertible he stopped, seeing something curious hanging off the rear bumper. At first, he thought it might be an old branch or something that got caught on the bumper as he was backing out of the wooded area. Then his heart jumped into his throat.

It wasn't an old branch hanging from his rear bumper.

It was a twisted *metal hook*.

The Killer

The woman had stopped at the gas station in the middle of the night, filing her tank up quickly and casting her gaze about her nervously. She went into the little convenience store, handed over her debit card to the tired-looking employee behind the counter, and said, "Have they said anything more on the news about that escaped maniac? The one that killed his family?"

The employee looked irritated, and said, "Lady, I been here all day, and we don't got no radio or television. How should I know?"

She frowned, said, "Yeah. Yeah, I guess you wouldn't know after all. Well, thanks anyway."

"Sure." The employee leaned over on his arm, lit a cigarette, and stared off out the door at the dark, rainy night. The woman quickly gathered up her change, put it in her purse, and headed out the glass doors into the parking lot.

She walked over to her car, clack-clacking her heels against the dark, slick pavement, when, suddenly, she noticed there was a car at the pump behind her. The dark shadow of the man at the wheel suddenly frightened her. Why wasn't he getting his gas? She fumbled to put her keys in the car door, and got in quickly. She put the keys in the ignition, turned them, and felt her heart sink.

The car was stalling. She tried it again, and still the engine was sputtering. She looked in the rear view mirror. The man in

the car behind her was getting out of his car, fast. He was approaching the driver's side window of her car.

She began to panic. She turned the keys in the ignition again. Suddenly, the engine roared to life. She thanked her lucky stars, and ripped out of the gas station parking lot, squealing her tires and heading out on the dark road.

The man hurried back to his car, got in, and started his own engine. It was a long, sleek-looking sedan, she noted, the kind of car a killer might drive. It was the car of a real villain. She was suddenly sure of it.

She drove a little faster. The man in the sedan sped up, following her, not even bothering to try and hide the fact. She sped up a little more, reminding herself that the roads were slick and that she didn't want to have a wreck. Every time she sped up, or turned a corner, or went down a different street, the dark man in the black sedan followed her closely. She could now feel her heart racing in terror.

She was soon running stop signs and red lights. The streets downtown seemed eerily deserted. Where were the cops when you needed them?

She continued to drive, speeding down dark side-streets and even alleys, always with the man in the dark car following her close behind. Soon, she was driving through her own neighborhood.

She didn't know if she wanted to lead this obviously crazy man to her own house, but she didn't know what other choice she had. She hoped that her husband would be home from work by now. She gunned the car, screeching to a halt, finally, in front of her own house, feeling her heart soar to see the comfortable light of the television set glow through the living room window.

Her husband, Bub, was sitting in his easy chair, watching the fights with a beer in his hand. He heard her pull up with a screech, got up quickly, cursing and spilling beer, and looked out the window, saying to himself, "Good Lord, doesn't that woman know any better than to drive like a maniac? She's gonna get herself killed!"

He looked out the window, saw his wife running up the driveway in terror, went to the door, flung it open, and dropped his beer on the rug as she leaped into his arms, saying, "Get your gun! This guy's been following me ever since I left the gas station. I think he's the escaped maniac on the news."

Bub looked over his wife's shoulder as the long, sleek. black car pulled up at the curb, and a huge, hulking man got out, hurrying like a hungry bear up the walkway toward his front door.

Bub went and got his gun.

"Now you just hold it right there, mister! I don't want to have to shoot you, but I will if you take another step."

The huge man, who was obviously out of breath from all the excitement, stood at the edge of the porch with his hands halfway raised in the air, and said, "No, mister! You got it all wrong. I'm not trying to hurt you or your wife. I followed her because I was trying to warn her. You see, there's a man hiding in the backseat of her car. I saw him crouched low when I stopped to get gas. I didn't want to say anything to her out loud, because I was afraid he might make a sudden move and kill her. All I could do was follow."

Suddenly, the three of them heard the back door of the woman's car creak open, and a bald head shot up from the backseat.

"See, there he is!"

The figure leapt from the backseat, and began running down the darkened street, disappearing into the otherwise peaceful neighborhood.

3

The Hitchhiker

Bill and his wife Jane were driving down a lonely stretch of old Indiana roads, coming home from visiting Jane's parents. It was an unusually foggy night, and for some reason, Jane didn't feel so good about the visit. Her parents were getting old, she reminded herself, and they didn't visit them nearly enough. One day, they would be gone, and then she would never have the opportunity to drive all this way out and visit them, ever again. The thought made her want to cry.

"Oh cheer up, will you?" said Bill, putting his arm around Jane's shoulders as she stared, gloomily, out the car window. "They're old, but they've still got a lot of good years ahead of them. It was nice a visit, and your Dad can sure tell some real whoppers. He tells some great stories."

"Yeah," she said, trying to cheer up a little. They were driving past an old cemetery. It did little to brighten her mood.

Suddenly, Bill said, "Hey, look at that. There's a girl standing at the shoulder of the road."

Jane stirred herself from her gloom. Indeed, just ahead, there was a teenage girl, clad in a white dress, standing at the shoulder of the road, just outside of the cemetery gates.

"Wow, we should stop and give the poor thing a lift, Bill. She'll freeze to death out here!"

"Yeah. And it could be dangerous for her to accept a ride from anyone but us."

Bill pulled the car up to where the girl was standing, staring gloomily off into the distance. Jane leaned her head out of the window, asked, "Hey, hon! Do you need a lift somewhere?"

Jane reached back and unlocked the back door. Without saying a word, the girl approached the car, opened the back door, and got in.

Both Bill and Jane noticed that it had become incredibly cold in the car, all of a sudden. But neither of them said anything, maybe putting it down to a sudden draft of the strange, cool weather. The girl was completely silent for the longest time, before suddenly saying, in a strange, hollow voice, "My name is Mary. I don't live very far from here. If you could, I'd like you to drive me home. My mother is waiting for me at home, and I'm late. She must be so worried."

"Okay. No problem," said Bill, a little nervously. Janet said, "I'm Janet. This is Bill. We're from Fairmount. Pleased to meet you, Mary."

The strange girl said nothing, and Jane turned back around in her seat, looking at her husband a little worriedly. This girl was, obviously, some sort of mental case, or something. She wondered if they shouldn't be driving her to a psychiatric hospital instead of home.

The girl gave very good directions, but said nothing else. It was a long trek down a number of old roads, cutting through lonely fields, until finally they came to an old weather-beaten farmhouse, with a wild, unkempt yard. At first, they thought the place must be deserted.

"Are you sure this is it?" Jane asked, with a little fear in her voice. The girl stared straight forward gloomily as the car pulled into the old dirt driveway and up to the rickety old porch.

Jane realized, all of a sudden, how strange the girl looked in her weird, old-fashioned dress, that must have gone out of style ten years ago. Also, where was her coat? Why had she gone out without it on such a chilly night? Suddenly, Bill said, "Hey, someone still lives here! A light just came on in the front room."

Jane turned to ask Mary why she had left the house without her coat. She felt her heart leap into her throat. "Bill!"

Bill shot his glance into the rearview mirror, then turned around in a fit of shock.

The backseat was now empty.

Mary had, seemingly, vanished into thin air.

Terrified and confused, Bill and Jane climbed the rickety porch in silence, and knocked, with shaking hands, on the old farmhouse door. It creaked open, and an aged woman suddenly appeared at the crack of the door. She didn't at all seem surprised to see them.

Bill didn't know where to begin.

"Hi, my name is Bill Black, and this is my wife, Jane. We picked up your daughter standing out near the cemetery a ways back, and she asked us to give her a lift home. Well, she's just vanished or something. I don't know how she managed it, but she snuck out of the car without making a sound, and now she seems to be hiding. My wife and I are really concerned about her. I mean, does she usually play this sort of trick on people?"

The old woman at the door smiled sadly, and said, "It's no trick, Mr. Black. This happens every year on this particular day. It's been like this for well over a decade. You see, my daughter's been dead for many, many years. She's buried in that cemetery where you picked her up. She's been trying to come home for a long, long time. I expect she'll try again next year."

The old woman seemed amused at the shock expressed on the faces of Bill and Jane. She said, "I apologize for any inconvenience this might have caused you. Hope you both have a lovely evening."

And with that the old woman closed the door, turned off the light, and went back to bed.

The Slasher

Darnell's mother was busy washing dishes, but her mind was far away. She was worried about her son. He had always been such a good boy, but now, it seemed like he was eager to get mixed up with Lavon Simmons and his crazy gang. Lavon was no good, she knew, and his family was always in and out of trouble. His uncle was doing a long stretch in prison for burglary.

Darnell had always been well-groomed, but now he let his pants droop in the rear, and he had taken to wearing his baseball cap sideways. She didn't like that one bit. She also didn't like the pounding rap music that came out of his room, disturbing the whole household. Also, his grades had started to slip downward. His last report card had had several *C*s and even a *D* on it. He had been a straight *A* student.

And where was he? He was supposed to be home for dinner by now. She shook her head. Ever since his father had died, Darnell had been the man of the house. Well, she knew that could be a lot to handle for a boy so young, but so far he had held up like a trooper. Until now. Until he met his new "friends."

She would be danged if she would let him go down the path she thought he was starting down. That path led nowhere, and she knew Darnell would be wasting all his potential. She would have a talk with him, alright.

She finished the last of the dishes, pulled off the yellow plastic gloves, and looked out the kitchen window. Creeping down the street she recognized Lavon's car, a beat-up old clunker that was usually crammed with his gang. Pounding rap music leapt out of the vehicle, making the car windows rattle and sending her nerves shrieking.

She watched in disgust as the passenger door was thrust open, and her son crawled out. He was wearing a big coat, droopy jeans, and his baseball cap sideways. He had started dressing exactly like Lavon and his friends, the whole rotten bunch that she knew were headed for trouble one day. The thought that her son was now trying to emulate and fit in with them made her feel disgusted from head to toe.

She heard the car creep away, heard the back door open and shut loudly, and heard Darnell try to creep past her in the hallway to his bedroom. Danged if she was going to let him off that easy tonight.

"Darnell!"

She heard him pause, turn around, and knew he was probably pretty scared that she was going to lay into him. And he had every right to be scared, because that is exactly what she intended to do.

"Yeah, Mom? Something wrong?"

He stood in the kitchen doorway, looking innocent enough, but she could smell cigarettes on his clothing.

"You've been smoking, haven't you Darnell? Gee, I never thought I'd have to worry about that with you, considering that that's what killed your father."

Darnell was quiet for a moment, then said, "It was just one cigarette, Momma. I swear. I'll never do it again."

She mumbled to herself, "Smells like a lot more than just one cigarette," but she let it go. Instead, she asked, "Where have you been at, Darnell? It's way past the time you were supposed to be home for dinner. Your dinner is in the fridge. Cold."

"I'm sorry, Momma. Me and the guys just lost track of time, hanging out and stuff."

"You and the guys, huh? You mean you and that no good Lavon Simmons and that gang of losers he has trailing behind him everywhere. I tell you Darnell, that bunch is nothing but

trouble. They're all headed straight to the same place Lavon's father is spending his days and nights. I think you know what place I mean, don't you Darnell?"

Darnell looked guiltily down at his shoes. He could never argue with the logic of his mother. Deep inside, he knew that she always knew what was best for him. But still, Lavon and the guys seemed so cool, and they seemed like they were depending on him to fit right in and become one of them. How could he let them down?

His mother bent close to him, softening her voice a little. "Look, Darnell. I want you to be honest with me, okay? Is Lavon Simmons in a gang? Does he want you to join a gang?"

His mouth fell open, and he closed it again just as quick. He could never hide the truth from his mother, no matter how hard he tried to keep a straight face. She always seemed to know what was on his mind, somehow.

Tears started to well up in his eyes. Deep inside, Darnell was a good person, and he knew he had no business hanging out with Lavon and his "boys." He knew that, in the end, it could only spell trouble. Still, though, it had been so good to be accepted, for once, and to feel like he was starting to fit in.

Darnell's mother pulled away from him with a very grave look on her face. She folded her arms, and said, "That's what I thought. Darnell, I thought you had better sense than to get mixed up with a crowd like that."

Darnell started to cry. "Oh Mom, I just wanted to fit in and belong! I just wanted to feel like I belonged somewhere! Anywhere."

He suddenly grabbed his mother tightly, hugging her and crying at the same time. Darnell's mother stroked his head, and said, "I know, baby. But being in a gang is the worst sort of belonging anyone can hope for. That way leads to prison... and even death, Darnell. Did you know that?"

He nodded, his mother still holding him closely. His face was still crammed into her chest, and he was fighting back the tears hard.

"Darnell, I want you to be honest with me. Have you joined this gang yet? I mean, are you a member?"

Darnell suddenly pulled away a little and looked up at his mother through bleary eyes. He shook his head no. She smiled. She could tell he was telling the truth this time.

"Good. Then Darnell, I want you to go to school tomorrow and tell Lavon and his boys that you can't hang out with them anymore. That you have studying to do. And church. And that they just take up too much of your time…"

"But Momma!"

"No buts, Darnell! Do as I tell you, or I promise you'll suffer a lot. Maybe not today, maybe not tomorrow, but someday. Hey, I want to tell you a story about gangs. About the stuff they make you do to become a member. Now, you say you're not a member yet, so they must not have gotten around to laying on you what's expected of you if you want to actually become a member of their gang. You see, Darnell, groups like that, they have what's called an 'initiation'. Do you know what that means, Darnell? It means you have to do something awful to prove your loyalty to the gang. Usually, they just beat you up, see how tough you are, and then you become one of them. After you get out of the hospital, that is."

Darnell felt his blood run cold. He was small, and he had never liked fighting. The idea of getting beat up and put in the hospital just so he could have friends seemed terrible.

Darnell's mother continued, "But, sometimes, they make you do something awful to somebody else. Some innocent person. Something that can get you in a lot of trouble. Do you think you're the type of guy that could hurt some innocent person, somebody that's just minding their own business? Did I raise you like that?"

"No Mom," said Darnell, wiping away his burning eyes. He was starting to get a clearer picture of Lavon and the guys now, and he wasn't liking what he was seeing one little bit.

"Of course I didn't. And you're a better person than that, Darnell. Too good to be hanging out with that bunch. Let me tell you a story of something that happened to your Aunt Agnes's friend, Betty. You remember Betty, don't you? She came to the family reunion last year. Anyway, there was this local gang, the Vipers they called themselves, and they had

a special initiation for new members. Do you know what that initiation was?"

"No Mom, I sure don't." Darnell felt like his head was swimming.

"Well, it was like this: When a new guy wanted to join the gang, he had to prove how much of a cold-blooded crook he could be. He had to prove how mean he was. So they would drop him off at a shopping center parking lot after dark, and have him wait underneath a car. With a switchblade knife in his hand.

"When whoever owned the car came out from shopping, the little punk would then crawl out and slash the ankles of the person before they got in the car. That's a serious injury, to the Achilles tendon, and the person would fall over. Then, they would rob the person of whatever they had just bought, and run across the parking lot to the getaway car. And that person would be injured for life, Darnell. Just think about it."

Darnell suddenly felt about two inches tall, but he was still fascinated by what his mother was telling him, so he let her continue.

"Now, as Aunt Agnes would tell it, her friend, Betty, had a son that wanted to join the Vipers in the worst way. And he was willing to do anything. And the whole family was really worried about him.

"So he went out to the parking lot, found a car he didn't recognize, climbed underneath it, and waited with his switchblade drawn. He waited, and waited, and waited…he was about to give up, when suddenly he saw a pair of feet come trudging along the darkened parking lot, carrying a few sacks. He couldn't see anything but the feet, but that was all he needed to see.

"As soon as he heard the keys rattling around in the door lock, he sprung out from underneath the car, and sliced into that poor person's leg, causing them to cry out in agony and fall over in a pool of blood. He then climbed all the way out from under the car, and started to grab the sacks when he got the shock of his life. The woman laying in a pool of blood, screaming for help, do you know who that was?"

Darnell could already guess. He had a lump growing in his throat, and he felt shaky all over, like he was going to be sick.

"That woman *was his own mother*, Darnell. That was Betty. He had forgotten that her car had been in the shop and she was borrowing the neighbor's car to do her errands and to do her shopping. You've noticed Betty walks with a cane? That's why."

Suddenly, Darnell's mother stopped and glanced out the window. The night seemed cold and dangerous beyond the kitchen window. She was glad her son was inside, safe and sound, and that she was getting the chance to try and talk some sense into him. Hopefully, it would sink in for good.

"So you just remember what I told you Darnell. And you remember that story, too. Now, when Lavon and his boys come up to you at school tomorrow and ask you to go "cruising" with them, what are you going to tell them? Just what decision are you going to make? Well, I want you to think about that. Now, go wash up, and I'll reheat your dinner."

The next day, Lavon and his buddies came swaggering down the hallway at school, and seeing Darnell, approached his locker.

"Hey Darnell, what's up man? Hey, you want to go for a ride with us at lunchtime? We got something we need to talk to you about."

Darnell was quiet for a moment, putting his books away. Lavon and the rest of the guys had surrounded him at his locker. He felt a little quiver of fear inside of himself, and then his mother's words came back to him:

No buts, Darnell! Do as I tell you, or I promise you'll suffer a lot. Maybe not today, maybe not tomorrow…but someday.

He suddenly swallowed his fear, turned, and said, "No thanks, man. I got to study up for that test next week."

Lavon looked genuinely surprised. He said, "Well, okay, how about after school then?"

Darnell made a disappointed face, and said, "No thanks, man. I'm gonna be real busy then, too. As a matter of fact, I don't think I'm going to be able to go riding around with you anymore, Lavon. I got school, and church, and a lot of other things to worry about right now. So..."

Lavon looked thunderstruck. He then looked really angry, as if he was about to start yelling and hitting Darnell. His gang started to mutter and close in, but just then a school security guard turned the corner and said "What seems to be the trouble here, guys?"

Lavon suddenly looked afraid, turned to the security guard, and said "Nothing. Nothing at all, man. We were just headed to class." He then turned to his followers, and they trudged off angrily, muttering to themselves.

Except for a few insults thrown his way by Lavon and his gang as they passed in the hallway, the lot of them pretty much left Darnell alone. And that was good. It left him time to become a straight *A* student again, to get more involved in his church, to find a girlfriend, and to be the sort of a son that would make his mother proud.

Darnell's mother had been shopping all day. She was proud that her son was doing so well now, and it seemed as if the talking-to she had given him had really worked wonders. She walked out to her car as the afternoon sun dipped behind a cloud. Her hands were full of grocery sacks.

Darnell's mother opened the car door, put her sacks in the back, and started to get into the driver's seat. Suddenly, searing pain shot through her ankle.

She fell backward onto the pavement!

A figure in dark clothes jumped out from underneath the car.

Darnell's mother and the figure in black exchanged glances before the figure ran off. Darnell's mother couldn't believe it. She was silent for a moment, barely able to believe who she'd seen running away. Then she began to cry.

5

The Bone Man

"The Bone Man will get you! The Bone Man will get you! The Bone Man will get you if you don't watch out!"

Shelly could hear the other children taunting her on the playground. They had told her a scary story, one that was sure to give her nightmares. She pressed her little hands against her ears and walked off to a corner of the playground to be by herself. She didn't like to be scared. Never liked horror movies, never liked Halloween, sure didn't want to hear anything about some guy called the "Bone Man."

Her friend, Ricky, was standing near the fence, looking out at the empty street. He seemed like he was lost in deep thoughts. Of course, Ricky was always a little weird; always really quiet. And he was shy.

"Hey Ricky, what you looking at?" Shelly asked.

Ricky thrust his hands into his pockets and spit a huge, green goober onto the sidewalk. A truck rumbled by, but before it was done clattering down the street, he had already started talking. He said, "It's true, you know. What they say."

Shelly felt herself suck in a little wind in surprise. She wasn't sure she wanted to know, exactly, what Ricky was referring to.

She found herself asking anyway, "What do you mean, Ricky?"

Ricky looked sad for a moment, and then said, "About him. About the Bone Man. He's real, Shelly."

Shelly wanted to slap Ricky and tell him to shut up and quit talking nonsense.

"Aw, Ricky, you're just trying to scare me. That's just a silly story they tell to kids they don't like. Kids they want to get rid of so they can hog all the playground equipment. Or because, like us, those kids just don't seem to fit in. So stop making up stories!"

Ricky had a far-away, weird look in his eyes. He said, "If you don't believe me, I can understand. But I'm not making up a story at all. The Bone Man is real. Real as you and me, alright. In fact, he use to live right here in this town. You see that old house down the street?"

Ricky turned all of a sudden and thrust out his skinny arm, pointing with one finger at a boarded-up old house about a block away.

Shelly thought it really was a creepy-looking old place. She wasn't very eager to hear the rest of this story, but she said, "Ricky, there ain't no such thing as the Bone Man, just like there ain't no Santa Claus and there ain't no Easter Bunny. My Mommy says that kids today are too…too…" Shelly trailed off, not being able to remember the word she was going to use.

Ricky said, "Sophisticated?"

The way he said it was as plain as day, and Shelly suddenly realized just how smart Ricky was. Maybe the smartest kid in the whole school. *Gee*, she thought, *maybe the Bone Man is real after all.*

"Yes, that's right, *phisisticated*. That's the word she used." Shelly couldn't quite wrap her mouth around the word still, but she thought she got it mostly right. "Mommy said kids today are smart enough not to believe in all that old stuff. I know I'm too smart for that. I'm a *A*-plus student."

Ricky looked sad for a moment, and thoughtful. He said, "Well, sometimes Moms can be wrong about stuff. Your Mom is wrong about this, and I'll tell you all about it. You remember Billy Johnson?"

Shelly shook her head slowly *yes*. Billy had been a nasty kid; a real bully. She had never liked him at all. Then, he just disappeared. Of course, some folks said it was because his parents got divorced, and his Mom up and moved to Michigan. But nobody really seemed to know for sure. At any rate, she was glad that he was gone: He had had flaming red hair, and flaming nostrils, and freckles, and a toad in each pocket, and always pulled her hair when she wasn't looking. He was the sort of kid that was always dirty and black and blue from being in schoolyard scraps. He had most always been in trouble.

Shelly wondered what Billy Johnson had to do with the Bone Man.

Ricky, who seemed even weirder today than usual, turned around again to the chain-link fence and pointed a finger at the old, boarded-over house, and said, "Up the hill from that house is a train track. You can't really see it from here, cause it is surrounded by trees and bushes and whatnot, but it's old and rusted and...evil."

Shelly searched her memory for the meaning of the word evil. Suddenly, a picture of a man in a red suit with a pitchfork, a curling moustache, a tail, and hooves like a horse popped into her mind. She said, in a low voice, "You mean, like the Devil?"

Ricky seemed confused for a moment, and then said, "Sort of. Not exactly, though."

Shelly felt herself get a little panicky. She said, "Mommy believes in him. She said he's the guy that makes people do bad things."

She felt a little bit of panic, now. Suddenly, a cloud seemed to darken the sky. In the background, she could hear the teachers yell that playtime would be over in five minutes.

Ricky said, "See, once there was this crazy old guy. Nobody knew what his real name was, or where he came from, but he lived in that old house down the street there. He had a bunch of dogs. And real long hair, too. Some people said he was an Indian. Other people said he might even be a witch doctor. Do you know what that is?"

Shelly shook her head *no*, although she thought that it was something scary.

"It's a guy who works magic. Bad magic. Yep. Sure does exist alright. Anyway, this guy was always walking around with a whole pack of mangy dogs. And he was always going down to the supermarket to get packages of old bones, for his dogs to gnaw on. You know, that's why some people started calling him that. Rick, the guy that works down at Jackson's Market, I think he's the one started calling him that. Long time ago. Anyway, he would sleep all day, and then go out roaming all night with those dogs. Nobody ever seen him do a day of work, or knew much about him. Older kids riding around at night would sometimes yell and throw stuff at him, like pop cans and stuff."

Shelly felt her stomach sinking a little. This was turning out to be an extra-scary whopper. If it WAS a whopper. Ricky looked as deadly serious as he could be.

"Anyway, he would get mad and shake his fist as they drove by, and kids said they could hear him yell things in some sort of funny language.

Then he would bend down and draw some sort of funny sign in the dirt by the side of the road. It was real creepy. The kids would drive back by and check out the funny symbol he made, and then they would get extra creeped-out, and get in their cars and zoom off quick."

Shelly was almost afraid to ask, but asked "Well, what happened to him?"

Ricky looked off into the distance at the old house. He looked up at the sky, looked for a minute like he was having some sort of fight going on inside his own head, put his hands in his pockets and turned around with a serious, scary look on his face. He said, "Well, that's the weird part. See, he was all the time with those old, mangy dogs. And one time someone saw him walking by and they said he was carrying a bag over his shoulder. And they said it looked like there was something in the bag. Like maybe a dead dog."

Shelly gasped. Ricky suddenly grinned a little.

"Only some folks said it didn't look like a dog at all. Some folks said it looked too big to be a dog. The folks that said they saw him carrying that bag one night swear up and down that it looked like the bag he was carrying had a dead body in it, or something."

Shelly gasped again, and felt her heart hammering away in her chest. She felt a little dizzy, and goosebumps were raised all over her arms.

Ricky continued.

"Anyway, some folks said that that was the reason the Bone Man never had to go to work. Because he would kidnap kids, and sell them to aliens to do experiments on at a secret base underground. You ever seen those milk cartons with the pictures of the missing kids on them? They say that's where those kids are at. All of them."

Shelly felt as if she might start crying. Her chin quivered a little, and she said, "Y-you stop making up nonsense, Ricky Joe Sanchez! No such thing ever happened. If you don't stop lying, I'm gonna tell!"

Ricky looked startled. He said, "I'm not lying! Honest I'm not. Anyway, even if I was, don't you want to hear the rest of the story?"

She started to shake her head *no*, but Ricky went on telling it, anyway.

"Well, all that stuff I just told you was rumors about him, you see. Nobody can say one way or the other. But one thing I know for sure really did happen was how the Bone Man done himself in. By accident. And that's where the story really gets good.

"You see, one night he had been drinking pretty heavy they say, and one of his dogs must have let loose on the floor or something, because he got mad and started whipping the old mutt. Or so they say. I heard it from Timmy Spencer, whose Mom's aunt heard it from her hairdresser, sure enough.

"Anyway, he started wailing on this poor dog with a stick and cussing at it, and folks said you could hear him up and down the street. The dog must have run out the backdoor and up the hill into the bushes, and so the old Bone Man followed, waving his weird stick and cussing in that crazy language that nobody could understand. He went right up the hill, drunk as a skunk, and into the bushes near the train tracks.

"Some folks say he passed out on the tracks from being drunk. Or that he had a heart attack. Or maybe he hit his head or something. Who knows? Anyway, he ended up passed out on the tracks. And a train came through that night. They found what was left of him the next day."

Shelly didn't feel like she could stand to hear anymore. Just then the teacher blew the whistle, and said, "Okay kids, recess is over! Line up!"

"I-I gotta go, Ricky." Shelly felt like her legs were wobbly rubber, the story had scared her so much.

Ricky suddenly popped an evil grin and said, "Wait just a minute! Here's the real kicker. You see, they say that if a kid passes that old place and stops to knock on the door three times, then that kid will hear a train whistle, low and creepy in the distance, and then the Bone Man will throw open the door and run out with his pack of dogs and swoop the kid up in his old sack. Then, that kid will be sold to the aliens who work for the government, and end up on one of those milk cartons at the supermarket. Say, want to see if that story is really true or not? We can walk over after school. I dare you! I dare you to call me a liar!"

But Shelley was already running away to join the other kids in line. Ricky smiled to himself, lingered at the fence for awhile looking at the old house, and thought, "What a clever boy I am."

As he was walking home later he passed the old place. It had a strange, broken-down look that made it seem menacing and weird.

Ricky walked down the cracked, uneven sidewalk, feeling his heart race a little in curiosity and excitement. Of course, he had made the whole thing up off the top of his head, but it was such a good story. Wouldn't it be cool, he thought, to just go up on the porch and try and peer through the dusty old boarded-over windows? He thought that it would. Of course, if someone saw him poking around, he might get in trouble. But it seemed so exciting. He couldn't resist.

He looked up and down the street slyly, before turning around and slowly walking up (on legs that felt excited and quivery) to the front porch. It was rickety and old and falling to pieces, and at first he was scared he might end up getting himself hurt. But he went up anyway.

He walked to the battered old door. There were several old, rough boards nailed across the front of the door, and it looked like someone had long ago tossed stones through all the windows of the place. Ricky leaned close to the old door, listening hard.

He heard something scurrying around in there. Probably rats, he thought.

No.

It sounded like something heavy. Maybe a big rat. Maybe the biggest rat of all time. Ricky found that his heart was pumping hard in excitement, as his eyes grew into big, bright circles.

He crept over the creaky old porch, to the boarded-up window, and tried to peer into the blackness beyond. He thought he could almost see something gray moving around in the darkness. He thought it might just be his imagination, though.

He walked up to the door, all shivery with excitement, and said to himself, "Nah! No way it could be real. I made it all up. Just a story to scare that little girl. No way there could be any truth to it."

But before he knew it, he had raised his little fist, and pounded on the door three times. He stood back, waiting for something to happen. When nothing did, he laughed to himself, turned around, and started back down the rickety old porch.

Suddenly, he felt a raspy, cold hand grab his wrist.

His heart froze in his chest, and a chorus of barking dogs greeted his ears as he whisked around to see the most horrifying figure he had ever seen in his entire life.

It was many days later, and little Shelly was following her mom around the supermarket. She hadn't seen Ricky in awhile (as a matter of fact, no one at school had) but rumor had it that he was sick at home with a real bad case of the flu. Anyway, Shelly had just about put that crazy story Ricky had told her out of her mind altogether. She decided he had just made it all up, and so there was no need to worry about the Bone Man, whoever he was.

She was pretty eager to get home and watch cartoons, and her mom had bought some of those slice-and-bake cookies.

"Honey," her mom asked, leaning over the cart as she pushed it along. "Do you want some milk to go with your cookies? Maybe some chocolate milk? Oh, but that wouldn't be very good with chocolate cookies, would it? Here…"

She leaned into the dairy section and retrieved a large carton of two percent milk, putting it down in the front basket of the shopping cart. Shelly smiled. She thought chocolate milk might go pretty well with cookies, as a matter of fact, but she knew her mother was worried the snack might be a little too rich for her. Anyway, a good cold glass of regular milk was also good with cookies.

Without thinking she turned the carton around.

She froze, suddenly.

There was a face on the milk carton, and underneath the word:

MISSING

Shelly couldn't read very well, but she knew what that word meant.

"Honey, what is it? What's wrong? Are you feeling sick?"

Shelly froze, looking at the picture of the boy on the milk carton. It was a long time before she could tell her mother all about the Bone Man and his strange, scary tale.

The Corpse

It was a "dark and stormy night."

I know that sounds like an old cliché, but it really was a "dark and stormy" night. We were driving along at a good clip, and I turned to Harold and told him, "Look, if you don't slow down, you're going to get us killed." Harold sat all hunched up over the steering wheel, his nose blowing steam on the windshield glass, and was still fuming over the argument we had gotten into at Dolores' party.

"Look, Harold, this is a road with a lot of twists and turns," I told him. "And it's dark and it's been raining. Will you please, for the love of Pete, just slow down!"

He suddenly came to a screeching halt, the car sliding all over the wet cement, and for one brief moment Mabel, I swear, I saw my entire life flash before my eyes.

"Harold!" I screamed at the top of my lungs, but the squeal of the tires probably drowned it out, and, at any rate, we stopped just short of going off the side of the road and into a ditch.

I turned around, picked up my handbag, and started hammering Harold in the side of his arm, saying "What! Are you trying to get us killed, you moron?"

Then I noticed Harold looking a little awestruck, as if he wasn't quite sure what had happened, and I followed his gaze out the windshield toward the skinny, rain-soaked figure standing illuminated in the headlight beams. Suddenly, a great flash of lightning lit the man's face in a weird, eerie strobe effect. And I actually gasped.

I had never seen a man so thin before. He looked like he hadn't had a bite to eat in weeks. His cheeks were all sunken in, and his eyes, too, and his whole face gave me the impression that I was looking at a skull with a thin layer of skin stretched over it. I actually gasped.

The man was standing at the edge of the road, and apparently had started to walk out in front of the car when Harold saw him and hit the brakes. Harold must have come only a short distance from running the man down. He looked like he was standing right in front of us.

He was also dirty, but I didn't notice it until he actually came around to the side of the car—the driver's side—and tapped on the window.

Harold nervously rolled down the window, ready to apologize for nearly striking the man down in the middle of the road, when all of a sudden the man cracked the most horrible grin you ever saw in your life, and with raindrops rolling down from the tip of his fedora cap and down his hollow old cheeks, he asked, "Hey Mister, pretty close call there. Mind giving a fellow a lift on a night like this?"

What else could Harold say? Harold, despite his gruff exterior, really has a heart of gold, although he'd hate for anyone to know that. Besides, what are you gonna do when the guy you almost killed just shrugs it off and asks you for a lift. And it was raining pretty hard.

"Sure thing, pal. Sorry about the...about that. I must not have been paying close enough attention. Hop in."

Well, the strange, skinny, dirty man got in, and right away I was worried about the upholstery in the backseat. How this old vagrant was sure to dirty it up. But I kept my yap shut, seeing as how Harold looked like another peep from me might get on his last nerve.

"So, what's your name, stranger?"

"I...I got no name."

Harold and I exchanged glances. Well, what do you say to something like that? Not only had we almost killed this skinny, dirty vagrant, but now he was in the backseat of our car, smelling the place up—and what do you know? He was a loon, to boot.

"Yeah," said Harold, sounding a little angry and a little frightened all at the same time, "Well my name is Goldberg. Harry Goldberg. This here is my wife, Estelle. Pleased to meet you..."

Harold trailed off, then said, "We can take you as far as the next town. If you want, I can give you a couple of dimes, you can get yourself a sandwich and a coffee at the all-night diner. If you don't mind me saying so, it looks like you could use a good meal."

And it smells like you could use a hot shower, too, I thought, but of course, I didn't say that.

And boy, did he ever stink! Like mold and earth dug up. Like he'd been playing around in the dirt at the side of the highway. I cracked the window, even though it let raindrops through, and suddenly realized how smelly the inside of the car had become since this guy had gotten into the backseat. Suddenly, everything was quiet and tense, the only sound the patter of rain on the roof and the swish and splash of the windshield wipers sloshing back and forth.

Harold mumbled something and reached over to turn on the radio. For a minute, we could hear the sound of a spooky old organ, and we knew it must be one of those radio shows like *Inner Sanctum*. Well, all things considered, we sure didn't want to listen to that, so Harold twiddled the knob some more until he came upon some relaxing ballroom music. It might have been Tommy Dorsey, but I can't remember now.

Suddenly, a voice broke in. A newscaster was saying something about the war, but I didn't really catch it, and don't remember what it was because the next thing we knew, our hitchhiker in the back seat opened his bony, jack-o-lantern mouth and said, "You know, I'm the sort of man that is awful good at making predictions. And I have two of them to make right now."

He then went silent. So Harry said, nervous and angry, "Well? What in the world are your predictions?"

The man smiled that horrible smile again (I could see it as the lightning flashed in the rearview mirror), and said, "Well, I know when the war is going to end, for starters. Hitler's

going to do himself in, and the Russians will take all of East Germany."

And then he went on to tell us when the war was going to end, and we felt our mouths drop open in shock. This guy was really some sort of loon, to think the war was going to end so quickly. And his voice was really slow and weird, like a record playing at half-speed. Really deep all of a sudden, and dragging like he was half-asleep.

"And another thing…and this thing is a little closer to home. By the end of the night, you're going to have a corpse in the backseat of this car."

Suddenly Harry huffed angrily, brought the car to another screeching halt, and said, "Look Mister! We…"

Harry turned around angrily, but his face suddenly fell slack.

"Estelle," he said, quietly. His voice was choked. I had my eyes in my lap, but I could feel a powerful sense of dread well up in me all of a sudden.

"Estelle!" Harry said again, this time in a hoarse, strangled whisper. I looked up in the rearview mirror, gasped as I felt a bolt of shock course through me, and then turned in amazement and terror.

The backseat was empty. The Nameless Man had vanished as mysteriously as he had come.

We drove on in silence for a few moments, Harry's hands shaking on the steering wheel. He kept mumbling to himself, trying to make sense out of it all, but I could catch very little of it through the chattering of his teeth. Suddenly, around the dark bend, just above the crest of a hill, we saw a flashing light. It was an ambulance, parked next to what appeared to be a wreck.

For some strange reason Harry stopped, popped his head out of the driver's side window, and asked, "What seems to be the problem?"

The driver of the ambulance, who looked grief-stricken, said, "This fellow crashed into an old fence post and is hurt bad. My partner is in back trying to save his life. But I can't get the ambulance to start! Can't imagine what's wrong with

it, except whatever it is I can't seem to find a way to fix it. Mister, I've radioed for help but by the time they get out here, I'm afraid it's going to be too late! Say, do you think we could transport him to the hospital in your car? It could mean the difference between life and death!"

Harold didn't have to even think about it, and in a few minutes the two ambulance attendants had placed the man in the backseat, lying down. Then, one of them squeezed in beside me, and said, "My buddy will stay out here until they get here, and explain what happened. The nearest hospital is in Marion. And we better step on it! This guy is losing blood fast!"

Sure enough, Harold did step on it, and I felt my knuckles go white several times as he made screeching turns and flew down rain-slicked roads, trying to make it to the hospital in Marion. All the while, the fellow in the backseat lay as quiet and stiff as a board. I was worried that he was gonna bleed all over the upholstery, and it turned out that is exactly what he was doing.

Finally, we saw the lights of the city in the distance, and we hightailed it downtown until we finally found the front entrance of the hospital. The ambulance attendant motioned us over to the curb, jumped out of the car, flew through the doors, and came back out only a few moments later with a couple of nurses and a stretcher.

They opened the door, and it was only a few seconds later that they had him up on the stretcher. The nurse tried to get his vital signs, but then suddenly put her hands to her lips in shock. The man laying on the stretcher was obviously dead.

We had both gotten out of the car and were standing at the curb. Harold turned to me, his chest heaving in and out in shock, his arms hanging straight down at his sides like he was wearing a pair of six-shooters and was about to grab for them. I could tell he was really startled.

He turns around to me and says, "When did that guy say that the war would end?"

Spiders!

Denny use to be such a good kid. Which is why, quite frankly, I don't understand what happened to him. I think it maybe had something to do with him just getting sick and tired of all the time being so good, you know? It was just like he started to snap a little bit around the edges. After that, he got weirder and weirder...

For instance: He started dying his hair strange colors. Pink, blue, purple...at one time he had it looking like a regular rainbow. Kids use to make fun of him until he started wearing spiked wristbands and scary t-shirts to class. And then came the patches: all over his pants and jackets, which usually were also adorned with safety pins and buttons of various punk rock groups. The stuff was often ripped, and rarely was it ever washed. He started walking around with this cloud of funny smell around him, and kids at school took to calling him "stinky."

And then he got his ears pierced. Then his nose. Then his lip. His mom and dad started bugging out at him because his grades began to fall. He started skipping school pretty regularly, and he started hanging out with a bad crowd, tough guys who were never going to amount to a hill of beans. His teachers began to send him to the office some days, and the school principal flat-out asked him If he was on drugs or in a gang. He blew up and stormed out of the principal's office, which cost him several days in school suspension. His mother wondered if she should send the kid to a shrink.

When he was home, he was upstairs in his room, which was littered with trash and empty food wrappers and pop cans and which had posters and flyers of bands like The Ramones and The Exploited and others covering every square inch of wall space. He would turn the stereo up, and his dad would sometimes yell at him to turn it down as he stood at the bottom of the stairs.

Denny usually ignored him unless he came to the door, and then he would get up and go to the door, and look at his dad like he was crazy. Then he would turn it down a bare notch.

One time, the neighbors complained, and someone called the cops. The officers came into the house, and Denny's dad angrily pointed at the stairs. They went up, walked in, and Denny must have flipped seeing two cops in his bedroom, all of a sudden.

They must have given him a heck of a talking to, because he quieted down and even seemed to improve for a little bit. He started taking regular showers and washing his clothes, and even shaved off all the strange hair he had colored and spiked into weird shapes.

It didn't last, though. Just as soon as Denny started hanging out with his new "friends" again, he started to change back to his old ways. In fact, he was even a little bit worse, and he started growing back his hair into the same porcupine quills he had cut off before. Now, he was into even harder and faster bands, stuff that didn't even sound much like music, and he got his first tattoo.

"Denny!" I remember his mother crying out when she first got a glimpse of it. "What have you done to yourself?"

"Aw nothing, Mom. I just...want to be myself, that's all."

His mother didn't look like she understood what he was talking about, and said, "I can't believe you would mark yourself up like that! Is that what you think you need to do to 'be yourself?' You just wait until your father gets home, young man, and gets a look at that! And who gave you that anyway? You know you aren't even legally old enough to get a tattoo!"

Without answering, he stormed up to his room and slammed the door. A few minutes later the music came on as loud as

ever, and I beat a hasty retreat, knowing that Denny's dad was due home any minute and that the stuff was really going to hit the fan then.

I remember the time Denny had a bunch of older guys in a pickup truck come by and harass him, too. It was scary stuff. They drove up, loud country music pouring out of the coach, and they started calling him all kinds of names. Stuff I won't repeat here.

Anyway, he must have flipped them the bird or something as they drove by, because all of a sudden they turned around and got out of the truck. They were big and smelly, and wore jean jackets with the arms ripped out and flannel shirts, and the driver was missing teeth. They looked like they probably worked at a local garage.

They both had enormous muscles covered in fading tattoos and hair slicked back like Elvis Presley. The driver seemed to be chewing a heavy cud of tobacco slowly. He spit, said, "You got yourself a problem, boy?"

Boy did those two ever smell. Denny was shaking in his boots, but he said, "No man, I got no problem at all. I was just waving at you."

The driver crossed his big, brawny arms over his chest and said, "You sure do have a funny look about you. Say, are you aware that Yves Tanguy sported a very similar hairdo during the heyday of the original Cabaret Voltaire?"

His friend suddenly piped up, said, "Oh man, you done did it now, man. You got him started on the early Surrealists."

His friend seemed irritated suddenly, and said, "Well not all of us are sold on classical modes of beauty and expression, Daryl. One should be more open-minded at the beautiful and vivid expression of the subconscious mind..

Well things went on like this for awhile, with Denny getting weirder and weirder as time went on. He started hanging out in graveyards and sleeping in abandoned houses when he got in fights with his parents. And he started going to these punk rock shows, and would come home all beat up, and be sore as all get out the next day.

Well, one day Denny was sitting in class, his hair a big, sticky, orange and green porcupine mess, and all decked out in his

jacket with the studs and spikes and chains. Nobody wanted to sit by him, cause everyone talked about how bad he always smelled (and he did smell bad! Hoo boy, did he ever!)

Jenny, the girl that sat next to him, was as straight-laced as they come, and she didn't like Denny one little bit. She leaned over on her one hand, trying to get away from his smell I guess, and looking like she couldn't wait for the bell to ring.

Denny must have fallen asleep. He was leaning over on his arms, but his huge porcupine hairdo kept getting in the way, and he kept having to shift now and again. Mr. Frecker just droned on and on about some stupid war a hundred years ago, while tapping back and forth from one end of his desk to another. He suddenly stopped, cleared his throat and said, "Denny? Denny!"

The entire class turned their attention on Denny, who sprang upright as if in surprise. One girl in the back of the class said, "Oh, he's sooooo gross!" in a kind of loud whisper, and a few people giggled. Denny looked at Mr. Frecker with a startled expression, like he had just been jolted awake after an hour of sleep.

And then something funny happened.

"Young man," said Mr. Frecker with a little nasty sound in his voice, "sleeping in class is not permitted."

Denny opened his mouth as if to say something, when, all of a sudden…something weird happened.

He begin to scratch at his clothes.

His face.

His spiky, multi-colored hair.

He suddenly fell out of his desk, and began rolling around on the floor. He was jerking around and yelling like a madman! Mr. Frecker stood there for a minute like a dummy, not knowing if this was just Denny playing a trick on him, or if he was really having some kind of seizure.

Someone in the back of the room said, "Aw, he always acts like this!" and a few people giggled.

Suddenly, the girl that sat next to him (who, like everybody else in the class, had their eyes planted on Denny as he wriggled and screamed on the floor), looked over at his desk,

and let out the most shrill and piercing scream I've ever heard in my life. It got Mr. Frecker moving over to the phone, and calling the office.

"Spiders!" she screamed. "Spiders! Spiders! Spiders!"

And then she threw up!

She was right, too. There were spiders crawling all over Denny's desk. Little ugly red suckers. They were everywhere! All over his desk and seat and book bag and crawling off across the floor. All the girls got up out of their seats and backed toward the walls, screeching. Truth be told, some of the guys did, too.

And a few guys and gals thought it was cool and actually moved closer.

They regretted that they did that later, though, I can tell you.

Suddenly, Denny stopped twisting around on the floor like a crazy man and sat up with the strangest look on his face.

Blood was trickling down his forehead. In fact his whole weird, spiky, colored mess of hair was now dripping blood.

And then it happened.

It was an explosion.

It was like a bomb went off in Denny's hair.

I swear it even made a sound, like a pillow exploding. I know that sounds weird. But it was loud and muffled, somehow, at the same time.

Only it wasn't pillow feathers that came flying out of Denny's hair. It was thousands and thousands of those ugly, crawly, evil little spiders.

The whole class went up in a chorus of screams as they just about trampled each other to get away. People were clawing at their skin, and the security guards came rushing in, but they couldn't believe their eyes.

And neither could I, to be honest.

Thankfully, no one else got hurt by that swarm of spiders, even though a lot of kids were rushed to the hospital afterwards, and a few of them had to have therapy later. Mr. Frecker took a long vacation, I heard later, and went to Florida for awhile and became a beach bum. But he finally came back to teaching!

Denny wasn't so lucky. The nasty little insects had, apparently, burrowed underneath his skin and laid eggs. Millions of them. Went straight to his brain. Yep, he was pretty much DOA as soon as they got him to the hospital.

Tabloid newspapers at the supermarket went on about it for a few weeks, with front page pictures that showed some clean-cut kids with huge spiders crawling out of his ears and headlines that read: MUTANT "SPIDER BOY" HAS HEAD EXPLODE! But the doctors figure he must have just gotten some spider eggs in his punk rock hairdo, and then a whole colony developed on Denny's head.

At his funeral, a few of his punk rock friends showed up to pay their last respects. They were all decked out in painted leather jackets with studs and spikes, and had tattoos and about a hundred piercings each, and their pants were all patched together with stenciled patches from different bands. And they all smelled terrible!

It gave the funeral director the creeps.

Anyway, to top it all off, they played Denny's favorite song right before they closed the casket for the drive out to the cemetery. And you want to know something? It was pretty appropriate.

It was by The Ramones. It was their cover of the theme song to the old cartoon version of "Spider Man."

(Now some of you may want to know how it is I know all this about Denny and what happened to him. Well, that's easy. You see, I'm the Narrator.)

The Babysitter

It was Halloween, and Sarah was excited.

Jake, the hottest guy on the football team, was coming over to keep her company. They could have their own private Halloween party, snuggled up on the couch watching old horror movies. She smiled to herself as she hefted her schoolbooks and walked down the sidewalk to the Thompson residence. She was going to baby-sit the Thompson twins, Billy and Jimmy, while their parents went out to a business dinner.

She had met Jake in Study Hall, had liked him instantly. He was tall, good-looking, had blonde hair, blue eyes, a square chin and a great smile. He was so physically fit, it almost made her sick with envy. Of course, she was no slouch herself. They had started going out almost immediately, and she was certain that he would be the one to take her to Senior Prom.

She sighed and smiled as she crunched leaves beneath her shoes. Life was so good, and this Halloween night was going to be the best. She was sure of it.

She walked up to the porch of the Thompson house, admiring the beauty of the place, and knocked. Mr. Thompson, half a layer of shaving cream on his face, answered the door in a huff, and before she could say anything, he turned and yelled, "Honey, the babysitter is here!"

He then turned, hurried back to the bathroom without even greeting her, and disappeared into the gloom of the back

hallway. Sarah walked inside, a little unsure of herself. She didn't like Mr. Thompson, and knew that most people considered him to be rude and not at all friendly. She walked into the gloom of the downstairs living room, and suddenly heard the clack-clack of high heels coming down the staircase.

"You must forgive my husband," said Mrs. Thompson, who was dressed to kill and had an accent that made her sound like a gypsy from an old movie. "Hi, I'm Maleva. Connie Drake told me you were...highly qualified. She said she recommended you, very much." Maleva Thompson spoke in the slow, careful way of someone that had not grown up speaking English.

"Well thank you," said Sarah, not really sure what else to say. She reached out and shook Maleva's hand, noticing how cold her skin seemed. A moment later, she heard two pairs of feet come trudging down the stairs, and Maleva turned saying, "Now boys, be very careful when coming down those stairs. We don't want you to fall and have an accident."

"It sure is a lovely place you have here, Mrs. Thompson," said Sarah, because she didn't know what else to say.

"Oh, it has been in Fred's family for a long time," said Maleva. "We have done much renovating and...how you say? Ah, yes. *Remodeling*, we have done much of that also..."

Billy and Jimmy soon made an appearance at their mother's knees, each holding a shiny toy or object. Billy had a toy robot, and Jimmy was holding out a comic book, asking, in an excited little squeak of a voice, "Hey lady, will you read to me later?"

Sarah bent down and peered into the little boy's face. He was so cute. She smiled, saying, "Sure thing, hon. And I'll make some caramel corn for us, too. My name's Sarah. What's your name?"

"My name is Jimmy. I'm glad you're going to be our babysitter, Sarah. Billy is glad, too."

Billy didn't say anything, but began to chew on his toy.

Maleva bent down and made him take it out of his mouth. She said, "We should be back sometime after midnight. Their bedtime is eight o'clock. And no later. No matter how much of a fuss they kick up. Got that?"

She looked down at her children with an amused look. Sarah said, "I'll be sure they get to bed on time, Mrs. Thompson."

"Now, keep the doors locked, and don't answer for any strangers of course. Also, if there is any trouble, don't hesitate to call the police, for goodness sake. And then dial the hospital."

"Okay."

"And, also, you aren't expecting any visitors tonight are you? I understand this is a very important holiday for American school kids. I've left a big bag of candy for trick or treaters, but Billy and Jimmy can have only a few pieces each, I don't want them making themselves sick before they go to sleep. It will give them bad dreams."

Sarah bit down on her lip. Actually, she was expecting Jake to drop by and keep her company for a few hours. Of course, he would be gone before the Thompsons ever got back from the company party, but still…

She nodded her head in agreement to everything, and Mr. Thompson strolled into the front room, nodded his head at Sarah, adjusted his cufflinks, straightened his tie, and said to his wife, "Are you ready, hon?"

"Yes. Well, thank you very much, and be sure to let me know if any of these two little monsters misbehaves while we are gone. Okay, Mommy loves you both."

She bent and kissed each of them on the forehead, and then followed her husband out the door. Soon, they were both in the car, backing out of the driveway, and Sarah was left with the two children in the big, quiet house.

She played a game of Shoots and Ladders with the oldest boy, Jimmy, while the younger boy played with his toy trucks in the center of the living room floor, pushing them across the hardwood floor and making a sound that sounded like "Vroom! Vroom!" again and again. Soon, the sun began to dip below the trees outside, and Jimmy tired of the game. Sarah got up, tuned on the television, and flipped to one of the cable channels that was showing a monster movie marathon. She stopped on an old movie with Bela Lugosi, settled in to the

couch with the kids curled up beside her, and then decided she was getting a little hungry.

"Are you guys hungry yet? I could fix us some hamburgers and French fries?"

Both of the children agreed, with smiles and jumping up and down, that this would be a good thing, so she went into the kitchen and did just that. After they ate, she would make some caramel popcorn in the microwave, and by that time, the trick-or-treaters would probably be knocking at the door. She readied a big glass bowl of candy, and as she stood at the counter she could see a jack o' lantern burning in the window of the house across the yard. It was Halloween alright she thought, with a little smile. And it was getting darker outside.

The kids munched their food slowly, making half-moons of the hamburger sandwiches and crunching their french fries slowly. They both sat at their little table while they ate, and both of them looked every once in awhile at the television with interest.

So far, it had been pretty easy. She vegged-out in front of the old movie, which was something with Frankenstein in it and looked like it was at least sixty years old. It looked pretty phony, too. Bad special effects and cardboard sets. She got up and went into the kitchen to make the microwave popcorn. Suddenly, there was a little knock at the door, and she rushed out into the living room, opening the door wide.

"Trick or treat!" yelled a foursome of little ghosts and witches. They held out their plastic Halloween candy bags while their mother (or whoever she was) smiled proudly.

Sarah gave them each a couple of pieces and saw them on their way. Already, a parade of similar little witches and monsters and goblins were parading up and down the sidewalk with their candy bags, in twos and threes, their proud parents by their side. It was a little chilly, and the shadows were growing long in the setting sun.

Sarah looked at the clock. The kids were sitting in front of the television, mesmerized by the silly old monster flicks, and she went back into the kitchen for the popcorn. It popped up in no time, and she walked back out of the swinging kitchen door and set the bowl in front of the two. They greedily munched up the popcorn, getting the sticky stuff everywhere, and she knew she would have a mess to clean up later. But, right now, they were both about half an hour away from having to go to bed, and that was a relief.

Soon, she told them, "Okay guys, it's time to get in bed. Go get your pajamas on, and the one that gets his on first gets a special piece of candy. Okay?"

They grumbled a little at first, being pulled out of the trance the old movie had put them in. But their mother and father were always strict with them, and they didn't complain much, but went right upstairs. Sarah smiled suddenly; she wondered why Jake hadn't called yet. She had given him the number at lunchtime, and he promised he would call and be over as soon as she got the kids off to sleep.

She tucked both of them in, giving them each a piece of Halloween candy, and making sure that they sat up while they chewed the sticky chocolate. She then got the oldest one a drink of water, and tucked them both in, safe and sound.

She was about to say, "Nighty night," when Jimmy, the oldest boy said, "Could you leave the light on in the hallway, Sarah? Mommy always leaves the hallway light on."

"Oh. Okay. Well, good night guys. I had a real fun time. Happy Halloween, and sleep well, okay. If you need anything, just holler. I'll be right downstairs."

"Okay, Sarah. Good night."

She left the door partway open, and the hallway light on, and went back downstairs. Why hadn't Jake called yet? He said he had an errand to run right before he came over. She wondered what that errand might be.

She sat in front of the tube, flipping channels. Everything was monster movies and ghost stories on television tonight, and it sort of gave her a creepy feeling. All those horrible faces on the television screen, and all that spooky theme music. She had a few more knocks at the door, gave out some more candy, and waited for Jake to call. She was starting to get a little impatient with him.

Suddenly, the phone rang, startling her a little. She got up, went to the kitchen counter, picked it up and said, "Hello? Hello? Is this Jake?"

But it was not Jake. It was some weirdo on the other end. He was breathing heavily into the phone, and saying nothing. It made her skin crawl, and she was suddenly mad and scared at the same time.

"Creep!" she said into the receiver angrily, and slammed the phone down. She felt her heart race a little, but reminded herself that it was Halloween, and people, kids maybe, were in the mood to play creepy pranks. She went back to the couch and sat down with a sigh. The evening was shaping up to be a little depressing. She flipped a few more channels, until she found a program where some maniac was stalking kids at a summer camp. She watched a moment of that before switching the channel quickly. She wasn't in the mood for that sort of thing right now.

Suddenly, the phone rang again, this time making her jump near out of her skin. She glanced out the window before getting up to answer it, noting that it was fully dark and the street was almost deserted of trick or treaters now. She went to the kitchen counter, picked up the phone with a trembling hand, and said, "Hello? Hello? Jake, is that you?"

But it was The Breather again. This time, he said a few strangled words:

I can see you standing there in the kitchen, and I know you're alone with the children...Sarah.

Sarah felt her blood turn to ice. This creep knew her name! She slammed down the receiver and backed away from the telephone, her thoughts racing, sudden fear gripping her. That didn't sound like a simple prank call. That sounded like a threat from some maniac. She wondered for a moment what she should do. On the television, a hideous space monster jumped out at a group of stunned scientists in long white coats, knocking over test tubes and beakers, and weird, frightening theme music filled the room.

Sarah grabbed the phone and dialed the police. She didn't use the emergency number, not really knowing if it was an emergency or not, but she got a very helpful person on duty who treated her with a lot of respect.

"I want to call and report a series of prank calls. This weird guy has called a couple of time now, and the last time he knew my name and said he could see me. I'm at the Thompson residence babysitting, and I'm all alone here."

The dispatcher on the other end said, "It may be some friends of yours from school just trying to scare you. It is Halloween, after all. But I tell you what: I'll trace the call and see where it's coming from, okay? Can I put you on hold?"

"Sure," said Sarah, starting to feel a little bit better. She glanced around at the doors and windows. It was really dark outside, and she suddenly felt very lonely and afraid when she thought about that dark, chilly night just outside. Oh, if only Jake had called or stopped by like he had promised he would, she would feel so much better. Jake was strong and protective. She knew he would make mincemeat out of any creep who tried to cause her or the kids any harm.

She heard the sound of music on the telephone, and glanced over at the television screen. Now, a legion of what appeared to be zombies were marching across the countryside. It was an old black and white picture. One of the zombies stopped and ate a bug off of a tree. *Gross*, she thought. Suddenly, the music at the other end of the phone stopped and the police dispatcher came back on. She sounded excited.

"Hon, I want you to listen to me very carefully: Get out of that house now! We traced those calls. *The man making the calls is doing it from the phone upstairs.* We're sending a squad car right away!"

Sarah suddenly dropped the phone, backed away from the counter in terror, her mind racing. There was a mad man upstairs! With the children! What should she do?

She could hear the dispatcher on the other end of the phone saying "Hello? Hello?" as the phone swung back and forth from its cord. She knew that the police would be here within minutes. But what if that monster did something to the

children? She couldn't bear the thought of just running out and leaving them, with that maniac intruder waiting upstairs to do whatever he wanted. No. She was better and braver than that. She would go upstairs and rescue the children, and hope that the police got there in just the nick of time to back her up.

She went to the kitchen cupboard, found the biggest butcher knife she could find, and slowly made her way to the foot of the stairs. The movie theme music on the television now was pulsing and nerve racking, sounding like the sort of music that is played right before a mad movie monster jumps out of the darkness to attack. She went to the bottom of the stairs, held the knife up near her shoulder, and begin to climb the stairs on legs that felt like they were made of rubber.

She climbed a few steps when, suddenly, she realized that the light upstairs had been turned off. In the trickle of moonlight coming from one of the bedroom windows into the hallway, she could see a vague, hulking shape suddenly appear at the top of the stairs. Her heart hammered in her chest in a mixture of fear and anger.

The hulking shape was wearing a cheap rubber mask. In one hand, he was carrying a knife. It was dripping blood.

Suddenly, with a scream of fury mixed with terror, she raced up the stairs at the creep, swinging her knife over her head, and stabbing him just below the shoulder. She knocked him back with the force of her blow, and they both tumbled over at the top of the stairs.

Her heart racing inside her chest, she suddenly realized she was laying on top of him, and jumped back, scooting as far away from him as she could. She could barely catch her breath.

The guy was bleeding badly. The knife was stuck in his chest, just below the shoulder. He moaned in pain. Suddenly, he brought his hand up and pulled away the cheap rubber Halloween mask. He raised his head and looked at Sarah.

She gasped in horror and amazement.

It was Jake.

Pop Goes the Freshman

Hey, I know you guys have heard this one before, but I swear to all the spirits above it really happened; back in the Eighties, when I was still in high school. You see, back then, they had this weird candy they were marketing to kids. It sort of popped and sizzled and exploded in your mouth. It tasted pretty sweet, too. It was good stuff.

Well, it really caught on like a fad at our school. Everybody was all the time walking around in the halls with a little plastic baggy of the stuff, just carbonated sugar, was all it was. But it came in different colors and flavors, and I think that appealed to a lot of kids.

Anyway, there was a rumor going around that you weren't supposed to eat the stuff and drink soda pop at the same time. Yeah, really peculiar. Don't know how that got started, but sure enough, we had a bunch of kids that were afraid to eat those crackling candies and drink soda at the same time.

Except for this one snot-nosed kid, Billy. Billy was a real know-it-all for a Freshman. Seems he was in the "Talented and Gifted" class, was every teacher's pet, hall monitor…the whole nine yards. Really thought he was something, that guy.

Anyway, he thought he was a real whiz when it came to science and stuff, and so one day during passing period, we were all standing at the lockers, me and Victor and Rick, and John might have been there, too. Anyway, we each had a baggy of those candies, and a soda pop, and each of us was daring the other to drink some pop, and then eat those candies.

"C'mon you chickens! What's the worst that could happen?"

Rick taunted the lot of us, but, as stupid as I knew the rumor to be, I still wasn't going to be the one to find out whether or not drinking soda and eating that popping candy would actually kill you. I mean, I had heard from a friend of a friend's neighbor that a kid in Peoria had done just that, and had dropped stone dead.

"No way, Man. You're so brave, why don't you try it?"

Just then, up came Billy, with his big glasses and his pocket protector and his arrogant know-it-all attitude. Oh man, I can still see the scrawny little guy with his curly red hair, freckles, his scrawny neck...Just like it was yesterday.

Anyway, he starts telling us all about how it is "scientifically impossible," that eating candy and drinking cola at the same time would lead to someone actually dying. Said it was just some stupid rumor, and that no one should be scared to drink soda pop and eat that exploding, crackling candy at the same time. Said it was all just carbonated water and sugar, and couldn't do any harm to anyone.

Rick smiled, held out the baggy and soda pop, and said, "So go ahead and try it, Billy, if you're so brave and so smart. C'mon, I dare you! You're not chicken, are you?"

Billy looked pretty mellow about the whole thing, and said, "Not at all. Here, give them to me."

And with that, he took the bag of candy, and dumped it all in his mouth, and then took Rick's soda, and drank it. All of it, if I recall. He then smacked his lips, and said, "Ah! Refreshing!" He wiped his mouth on his sleeve. Come to think of it, Billy actually had some pretty gross manners, now that I remember.

Anyway he stood there a moment, and there were people still passing by in the hall, but the bell was getting ready to ring. All of a sudden, I'm looking at Billy, and he's not looking so good. In fact, he's turning a peculiar shade of green. And,

to top it all, he has this weird kind of foam that starts seeping from his mouth. Looks like he's belching up shaving cream.

Rick started to laugh, along with the rest of us, but our joy was short-lived. Billy looked, all of a sudden, really bad, and his face started to swell. I mean, swell up in a matter of seconds.

We were stunned into silence, but just then the bell started ringing and everyone dashed for class. Except for us. We were too intrigued and worried about Billy to do anything but stand there and stare at him.

Billy dashed, too. He dashed across the hall straight for the Boy's Room, just as the smokers and heavy metal guys were coming out, trying to fan themselves off lest the principal should notice the smell.

Then, just as the bell stopped ringing, we heard it. Sounded like a cannon went off in the Boy's Room. I mean, you could have heard it a mile away. Despite our fear we raced inside.

Just behind us was a teacher that just happened to be passing through the hall nearby. She followed us through the door.

We all screamed. It was like a chorus of screams, really. It brought everyone out of class and running down the hall.

They say the teacher was forced into retirement after that. Say she had to spend time in a nuthouse to get her mind straight.

As for me, I'm a pretty tough guy upstairs. Very little bothers me. I mostly just try and forget about that day, and the horrible thing I saw splattered all over the walls of that bathroom.

So, take it from me. If they ever bring that candy back out on the market, do not make the same mistake that Billy made so many years ago. Because sometimes even a know-it-all can be proved deadly wrong.

10

Earwigs!

Jenny had a strange itch when she woke up. It seemed like her ear was tingling and throbbing, and she quickly got up, went to the bathroom, and tried to rinse it out with some water. It was no use. She reached into the medicine cabinet and pulled out a box of cotton swabs and some peroxide. She dabbed the end of the cotton swab in the bottle of peroxide, and started to dig around in her ear.

Ouch! Man it was sore. Felt like something had gotten in there and was wiggling around. She wondered if she might have some sort of strange ear infection. Considering how careful she was to always take care of her health, she couldn't imagine how she could have possibly gotten any sort of infection at all.

Her ear was burning and itching, but she knew if she dawdled anymore she would be late for school, so she did the best she could to ignore the pain, hopped in the shower, and was extra careful to wash her ear out with soap. Then, getting out and toweling herself off, she reached into the medicine cabinet and pulled out a little brown bottle of the stuff she used when she had had ear infections in the past.

She looked at the label. The prescription was outdated, but she hoped it might still be strong enough to do the trick. She quickly took another Q-tip, dipped it into the pungent-smelling stuff, and daubed some around in her inner ear.

Then she went to get dressed, careful not to scratch her ear, lest she make it any worse. The itching and pain seemed to subside a

bit, and she quickly went out to catch the bus, clutching her jacket around herself against the cold.

She got to school, said hello to a few friends standing in the hallway, and then went to class, careful to slip in just before the bell rang. Her first class was Trig, which she hated, and her ear really started itching badly while the teacher, Mr. Krabbe, droned on and on, scratching chicken-marks on the dusty old board. The room was awful hot; it seemed like ever since winter had come on, the school was doing everything it could to make sure that everyone stayed nice and toasty. She yawned, reaching up once again to scratch her irritating ear.

Her next class was History, which was a little better, but still far from being her favorite subject. Man, her ear was really driving her crazy now. It was all red and swollen. She couldn't seem to stop scratching it. She was afraid she might scratch it until it started bleeding.

"Jenny? Something the matter?"

"No, Mr. Baker. Just…I think I might have something wrong with my ear! It itches and burns awful bad."

Someone piped up from the back, "Jenny has cooties!" There were a few snickers, and Mr. Baker shot a kid in the back an ugly glance.

"Would you like to go to the nurse? I could write you a pass."

She perked up a little.

"Oh, would you, Mr. Baker? That would be great. I'm really not sure how I can concentrate with my ear like this."

Mr. Baker bent over the desk, got out his pass pad, and scribbled on it. Jenny walked to the front of the class, feeling just a little dizzy now, a little faint. She took the slip of paper, and swaying a little walked out of class, feeling dozens of eyes on her back.

She went down the hallway groggily, acutely aware of kids (why weren't they in class?) standing at their lockers chatting, and staring her down as she went past. They all looked at her like she was a total freak.

The hallway seemed to be a million miles long now, and her head felt like it was swimming. Each footstep was heavy, and her legs felt like they were made of lead. She didn't know if she was going to have the strength to make it to the end of the hallway, or

just pass out right there from exhaustion. And her ear was really hurting badly now.

She finally got to the nurse's station. The nurse, a young woman named Mrs. Florentine, took one look at her and said, "My dear, are you running a fever? Have the flu? You look terrible! Come in here at once, this very instant, and lay down!"

Jenny was led to the back of the nurse's station and shown to a leather sofa with a roll of paper on it. She sat down on the sofa heavily, leaned back, closed her yes, and passed out, hearing Nurse Florentine speaking excitedly on the telephone.

She opened her eyes momentarily, feeling the itch on her ears, and realizing now that it, seemingly, had spread all across her body. She began to scratch herself, suddenly realizing why it was she was itching so badly.

She pulled back her hands and they were covered in bugs!

BUGS!

She was crawling with little brown, crusty, itchy bugs! They were crawling through her shirt, her jeans, her socks; she seemed to be infested by them. She realized they were colonizing her hair and sweeping across her face and getting in her eyes.

She began to claw at herself, frantic to be free of the bugs. Suddenly, she lost it, and screamed as loud and long as she ever had.

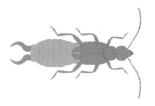 

She jerked awake, gasping for air. Her eyes began to adjust to the light. She breathed a sigh of relief. She had only been dreaming. She must have become delirious. Where was she?

Suddenly, she was comforted as she saw her mother and another man come into the room. He had on a long white coat, and there was a stethoscope around his shoulders. He had on a really silly tie with teddy bears on it.

"W-where am I?"

She had actually already guessed she was in the hospital.

Her mother said, "It's alright dear. Everything is going to be alright now. You had…a little problem with your ear canal, and it made you dizzy. But we think we've taken care of it."

The doctor said, "That's right young lady. We had to bring you in here in an ambulance. You were out cold. This," and he held up a little jar, pulled out a pair of tweezers, and fished something out of it. "was the culprit. It's called an 'earwig.' A really nasty little bugger. They're rare, but they do actually exist, despite what some folks say, and sometimes they crawl inside your ear when you're sleeping. This one appears to have gotten stuck in your ear canal, and caused your ear to swell up, making you ill. We fished it out though, by golly!"

The doctor seemed to think this was amusing, and laughed out loud. He placed the little curled object in his tweezers back into the jar, and screwed the plastic cap on tightly, adding that it was "for his personal collection."

Jenny reached up and felt the bandage on her ear. It was uncomfortable, but they must have given her some really good painkillers, because she didn't feel the pain all that bad now.

"Now, young lady, I say you're lucky because this was a male earwig. And, we got it just in the nick of time, too. A male earwig will burrow its way straight through your eardrum and into your brain, and come out the other side. No joke. I've read about several cases in the medical literature. Now, once a male earwig eats through to the brain, the person stops feeling any pain, thinks everything is okay, and never even realizes what's going on until…You see, Jenny, the brain has no pain receptors, so it tunnels straight through and the victim never even realizes until one day, they just keel over. Stone dead." His voice grew grave and serious.

"But, boy, we got this little fella just in the nick of time, alright. Now, lucky for us he got caught in there and lost somehow, and lucky too that we got him before he found his way to chew right through your brain. Aren't we lucky we got him, Jenny? Huh?"

Jenny nodded vaguely, her mouth hanging open and her eyes wide as twin moons.

"Like I say, you always have to count your blessings. But we're also very lucky in another way, too. Do you know what way, Jenny?"

She started to shake her head *yes* slowly, and then shook it *no*.

"Well, like I said, analysis showed this to be a *male* earwig. Horrible enough, but not nearly so bad as if it had been a *female* earwig. Oh boy, those are the worst of the worst!"

He shook his head, whistled to himself, paused for a moment, and then said, "Jenny, do you know why female earwigs are more dangerous, more deadly than male earwigs?"

"No," Jenny said meekly.

"Well, it's because even if we had managed to fish the earwig out in time, and dispose of it in my little jar right here like this one," he held it up again until it caught the light, "if it had been a *female* earwig, it wouldn't have mattered one bit. The female earwigs, you see, lay millions of eggs wherever they happen to burrow into. You'd have been a goner, for sure, I'm afraid."

Suddenly, a young, handsome intern in a long white coat and snazzy tie popped his head in the door, and said "Doctor, could I have a word with you? You, too, Mrs. O'Reilly."

Jenny's mother turned to her, looked down, said, "You just rest easy honey. We'll be right outside the door in case you need anything."

The doctor and Jenny's mom went outside and joined the young, handsome doctor right outside the door, there was a slight whispering, and a pause, and then Jenny heard the words "...analysis...proved wrong...infestation."

She suddenly heard her mother give a choked sob, and the doctor moaned "Oh, no, it can't be!"

Jenny reached up and felt a trickle of blood fall from her nose. She thought she might still be dreaming.

Suddenly, the light grew dim, she felt the room begin to spin, and before she knew it the world around her faded to black.

11

The Hippy Babysitter

Bill and Jane Crockett were very happy this evening. Bill had been awarded two tickets to the hottest show in town because he'd answered a question on a call-in radio program correctly. The show, which was an experimental opera performed by musicians using homemade instruments, was actually being held in a pretty ritzy theatre. Which surprised Jane, who figured shows like that were usually only held in seedy clubs full of smelly punks and people with pierced faces.

Bill was excited. Heck, they had never dressed up to do anything very "cultured" or classy, and the last time they'd even attended anything together had been a high school basketball game. Bill made sure to wear his best suit, and Jane spent all evening getting ready, fixing her hair and makeup and daubing on enough perfume to send a room full of people climbing the walls. Bill sniffed, thought she had put on too much, but was too nice to tell her that she had overdone it. Anyway, he didn't want to ruin this particular evening.

Of course, they couldn't take the baby with them, so Jane had phoned Millie, the old lady next door who kept a bunch of cats but who worked as an attendant on a school bus, and who knew all the girls that did babysitting. She gave her a number of a girl named Rhonda. Jane called Rhonda, but Rhonda said she, like, just didn't have the time tonight, or something.

"Any luck yet with a babysitter?" asked Bill, straightening his tie.

"Nope. It's Friday night, and you know how teens are. But Rhonda gave me the number to this other girl. But she seemed kind of funny about it. Anyway. I'll give it a try. If we don't find someone soon, we're going to end up missing the thing!"

"We could call your mother," suggested Bill.

"No, we can't," Jane scolded him. "Mom hasn't been feeling well lately. In fact, I'm kind of worried about her. I can't call her up at the last minute and ask her to come over and watch the baby. Why, the woman would go bonkers…"

"She's already bonkers," Bill smirked.

"Hey, that's my mother you're talking about, Mister!" Jane shot back. She sighed, picked up the phone again, and dialed the number of the girl that Rhonda had suggested. It rang and rang, but finally a groggy-sounding voice on the other end answered, saying, "Like, hello? Like, who is this?"

In the background, Jane could hear some groovy rock music that sounded like it was about thirty years old. Maybe it was that band the Grateful Dead? She couldn't tell.

"Yes, this is Jane Crockett. I was given this number by Rhonda Fonda. She said she couldn't baby sit tonight, but that her girlfriend Melba might be able to come over and watch the baby while we go to the show.

"Melba? Melba?" said the voice on the other end, as if he had just woken up from a deep sleep. Suddenly he said, "Oh, you mean 'Orange!' Yeah, I plum forgot that her real name was Melba. Melba Toast is her real name. Kind of funny, isn't it?"

Jane didn't know if it was or not, but she asked, "Orange? Why do you call her Orange?"

The voice broke into hoarse, friendly laughter. The guy sounded about twenty years old. She could picture him with a scruffy beard, no shirt, little round glasses, and bell-bottom jeans with sandals.

He said, "Well, actually we call her 'Orange Sunshine'… you know, because her hair is so red it's kind of orange, and because she's always groovy like a ray of sunshine. Just… groovy, Mama."

"Don't call me that ever again!" Jane said angrily.

"Oh no," explained the young man at the other end of the phone. "I wasn't calling you that, honest injun. I was just using it as a beautiful expression of righteous harmony, you dig? You guys groove on harmony, don't you? I mean, you're not square or anything, or you wouldn't even be calling."

"Look buster," said Jane, starting to lose her patience, "just put Melba, or Orange, or whatever you call her on the phone with me if you could! My husband and I are about to be late, and we need a babysitter pronto. Can you dig that?"

"Yeah, yeah lady, just calm down. I'll go get her. I think she's in the kitchen with Charlie mixing up some fruit punch. We need the bread real bad right now, so I know she'll be interested in coming over and watching the tot. Hold on."

And with that, the young man put the phone down and she could hear him walking around in the background, and some muffled talking and then a man's voice said something like, "You'll do what I tell you to! We need the bread, woman!"

Suddenly, someone picked up the receiver and a sleepy voice said, "Yeah, this is Oran...er, I mean Melba. Sure, I can come over and watch the kid. Just give me a few minutes to get my stuff together, and...oh, what's the address?"

Jane told her the address. Melba said, "Oh hey, that's great. Not too far away, man. I dig that. Be there in no time at all." Suddenly, Melba yelled with her mouth away from the phone, "Bruce, I need me a ride out to the rich woman's place. Can I borrow the Bug?"

She then came back on and told Jane, "Yeah, everything is cool, lady. Be right over."

And with that, they were all set.

They waited. And waited. And waited.

"She's a beatnik freak," said Bill. "I don't think she'll show up at all."

"She'll show. They sounded pretty desperate for cash." But Jane was starting to have her doubts.

Then, just in the nick of time, the doorbell rang, and Jane rushed to open it. She goggled at the girl she saw standing before her.

She had incredibly long, straight black hair, black sunglasses, a brown leather coat with fringes that looked like something a cowboy in an old movie might wear, and a tie-dyed shirt. There was a headband decorated with strange designs around her forehead, and a huge peace symbol medallion around her neck. He jeans were bell bottoms with painted peace symbols on them and colorful strips of cloth sewn into the sides. And she was barefoot. And her feet didn't look too clean.

"Whoa, this is some pad you guys got here! It's really funky. I dig it. Oh, I guess I should put my sandals on and not get your carpet all dirty."

She had her sandals in her hand for some reason and took a long, slow time putting them on. She also had a backpack with patches and buttons and peace slogans all over it.

"Okay, um...well, I'll give you ten dollars. Okay? And the baby is asleep anyway. If he wakes up, he'll want his bottle. You can heat it up on the stove. He gets a little fussy sometimes, but you seem so...mellow, I doubt you'll have much problem soothing him back to sleep."

"Oh yeah," said Melba. "I'm a real natural with kids. We have lots of them here."

Jane didn't know what Melba meant by that comment, but let it go. Was she talking about living on some sort of commune?

Melba made herself comfortable on the couch, said "Wow, you guys have a color TV! Far out!" and Jane fussed with her hair for a few minutes before a few blasts from the horn told her that Bill was waiting for her outside. She turned, said, "Now, I don't expect there will be any trouble, but if there is, here's the number for the place where we'll be at. Just ask for the manager and he should be good enough to have an usher come into the theatre and get us. Now, if you get hungry, feel free to get what you want from the fridge, okay?"

And with that, Jane turned and clack-clacked out the door.

As soon as they pulled up to the place, they knew they were in for a wild time. For starters, it was packed. It seemed to be a

pretty upscale crowd, for the most part, but Jane noticed some weird-looking beatnik types that were standing in line, and she grimaced. They looked really dirty, and she snarled her nose up hoping they wouldn't be forced to sit next to them.

An hour later, and Jane felt like she could climb the walls. The music was terrible, and even Bill didn't seem to be enjoying it very much (and he usually took to anything that was odd or unusual). It really, Jane thought, couldn't even properly be called music; just a horrible rattling and banging on a bunch of trash cans that littered the stage, while half-naked actors stomped around covered in paint and yelled at the audience and blew through aluminum horns and broke stuff that must have had microphones attached.

And there was enough fog rolling from the fog machine to cut through the air with a knife. And horrible flashing laser lights and big rumbles and screeches erupting from the sound system at odd times.

"I think we must have died and gone to Dante's Inferno!" Jane yelled to Bill as he struggled beside her, trying to look as if he was enjoying himself. He wasn't doing a very good job of faking it, and replied, "I don't understand it! This show got rave reviews!"

What was worse was the crowd of loud, smelly young people dressed in black sitting one row over. They seemed like they were absolutely entranced by what was going on, and they all stank to high heaven. Jane wondered if maybe they wouldn't start drawing flies if they sat there long enough.

"Do you want to leave?" Jane shouted over the racket. She actually wanted to leave very badly. Bill looked around a little at the rest of the audience.

Amazingly, they all seemed like they were entertained and quite pleased to be there.

Jane hated the show. But she also felt an inexplicable fear suddenly come over her. Everything seemed wrong somehow, all of a sudden. They shouldn't be here, she thought to herself; they should be at home looking after the baby. All of a sudden she felt a twinge of panic grip her heart, and she wanted to be away from the loud, awful performance, which seemed like it was straight out of a nightmare.

"C'mon! Bill, we gotta get home! I got a bad feeling! I think I'm gonna be sick."

Bill didn't need much more convincing than this, and got up, heaving a gusty sigh. On the way out of the lobby, they passed the usher, who was standing with his hands over his ears. As they were going out the glass doors, they both noticed that the music had stopped, and they both realized that a huge, roaring applause was erupting in the theatre. Bill said, disgustedly, "I swear, you could make some people enjoy anything if you told them it was art!"

All the way home from the university theatre, Jane sat in the front seat of the car, nervously nibbling her fingernails. Something was wrong; she could feel it. She kept urging Bill to drive faster.

"Jane, if I go any faster than what I am now, I'm gonna wrap this car around a tree!" Bill finally said, angrily.

At last, they pulled up in front of their house. The lights were out, but Jane could see the glow of the television as she clack-clacked up the drive and through the front door.

Jane opened the door hurriedly, and found Melba sitting on the couch, cross-legged, as if she hadn't budged an inch the entire time. Jane smelled funny smoke in the air.

Melba turned, and Jane could see right away that she was as high as a kite. Her eyes were like twin burning coals (or, at least they seemed that way to Jane, at any rate), and she said, "Man, this show is…far out! I dig it."

Bill came through the door behind her, closing it angrily. He could see right away what was going on. On the television screen was a television network test pattern.

"Melba, have you been doing drugs in our house?" Bill asked angrily. Suddenly, Jane stepped forward, past the couch, and noticed some funny red stains on the wall. Had Melba gotten so high she started finger painting on the wall?

As if just realizing she wasn't alone, Melba finally said, "Oh hey, Mrs. C! You're already back! Far out! I think I must have had a flashback or something while you were out. Totally spaced it! Totally! Oh, I put the turkey in the oven."

Turkey? What turkey?

71

Jane suddenly noticed that paint trailed straight through the kitchen door, and she realized there was smoke coming from the oven. And a horrible smell that was making her instantly sick to her stomach.

"Turkey? But, we don't have a turkey!"

She then realized what the red splotches all over actually were. They weren't puddles of finger paint. She ran into the kitchen, threw open the oven door, and the next thing Bill heard was a horrified scream that seemed to last forever.

Jane fainted. Bill rushed into the kitchen and let out a scream that could be heard down the block. His mind could not possibly conceive of the insane horror he saw sitting in a huge broiler on the top rack.

Later, Jane would spend years in a mental institution before finally getting out, going on several talk shows, and writing a bestselling book. Bill grew his hair out, changed his name to "Lance Stanley," and became a producer of several top forty records, mostly in the "abstract sound" genre.

As for Melba, she was confined to a mental home, where she finally flipped out completely, imagined she was a glass of orange juice, and spent the rest of her life begging the staff not to drink her.

And the moral of this story? Never trust a hippy. Or, at least, a hippy babysitter.

The Boyfriend

Maddy and Mark were out on a really hot date.

The air-conditioning in the car was broke, and the window on the passenger side would only roll down partway, and it must have been eighty degrees out that night. It was really sticky, and the chili dogs they had eaten for dinner had given Maddy gas. It didn't seem to bother Bill any, who had turned on some romantic music (which she hated) and had snuggled up next to her.

"I want to go home!" Maddy said, feeling a little irritable and gassy.

"Oh come on babe!" Mark said, feeling a little let down now. He had driven out here to Lover's Lane, and it was a really beautiful night for as hot as it was. A big, beautiful full moon was shining down, sending slender shafts of light through the tree branches above. He wanted to stay out here all night smooching, but it seemed like Maddy was not really in the mood.

"It's creepy out here, Mark," she said, putting her hands on her arms and drawing them in close. "I'm cold."

He couldn't believe it.

"You're cold? I can't believe it! It must be eighty degrees out tonight!"

"Yeah, well, I feel cold anyway…got a problem with that?"

"You want I should turn the heat on?" He was actually sweating really badly, but he was willing to do anything to make her happy.

He suddenly cracked a big grin and said, "I'll warm you up, baby!"

He tried to pull her close but she pulled away.

Suddenly:

"What was that?"

Mark looked around, a little irritated, and sighed, "What? I didn't hear anything."

"I heard something out there."

"It's just the breeze making the branches rattle against the car. Nothing major, babe!"

"Uh, I could swear I heard someone walking around out there. Mark, I want to go home."

She suddenly sounded like she was going from being cranky to being panicked. He sighed, sat back in the driver's seat, and started to turn the key in the ignition.

Nothing happened.

"What in the world? I know I put plenty of gas in this sucker before we left!"

"What's wrong?"

"What's wrong? What's wrong? I'll tell you what's wrong: This sucker won't start!"

"You've got to be kidding!"

"No! I think it's the battery. Cripes! I knew I should have gotten the darn thing checked out before we left!"

"Oh, you've got to be kidding! Are you just doing this to keep me out here? C'mon, quit messing with me Mark!"

He turned on her suddenly, sweat pouring down his face, and said, "I'm not fooling around here Maddy! The car won't start! It's the battery! I'm gonna have to walk to a gas station, or something!"

Maddy suddenly cried, "No! Don't you dare go off and leave me alone here!"

Mark said, "So what, you want to spend the whole night out here or something? Well, all I know is you'll have to go with me, and it's a long walk. Are you ready for it?"

Suddenly, they both stopped talking as a kind of weird, shuddering scrape, long and loud, echoed out in the darkness. Mark could feel his pulse begin to race, and he said, "What...I think there's somebody out there. Wait. I'm gonna go check it out!"

"NO!" Maddy was starting to become hysterical, and she was getting on Mark's nerves.

"Maddy, look, if there's somebody out there, maybe they can help us. Maybe they're hunting or...who knows. Anyway, I need to get some air and think about things a minute. Wait here."

Before she could say another word, Mark popped out of the car, and turning around, leaned in the window, saying, "Just to be safe, roll 'em up and lock 'em 'till I get back. Okay? It sounds like maybe a hunter or something is out in the brush. Maybe he and his buddies will give us a lift home. At any rate, I hear some whispering out there. I'm a big boy. I can take care of myself."

Maddy felt like she was having a bad dream, and she bit the ends of her fingernails nervously. She said, in a trembling little voice, "Okay. Just, make sure you yell out or something so's they don't think you're a deer or something."

"Will do. Love you babe!"

"Love you, too, Mark. Hurry back, okay?"

"Will do!"

And with that, he disappeared into the darkness.

Maddy waited and waited, feeling her nerves grow more and more tense. She wanted badly to turn on the radio, but realized Mark had taken the keys with him, and then remembered that the car wouldn't start for her to use the radio anyway. What was taking him so long? It seemed like her nerves were on edge, and this horrible night would go on forever. She felt tears well up in her eyes, and her heartbeat was very fast.

She felt prickles of cool fear all over her body.

Suddenly:

Clump-clump.

She felt her breath catch in her throat. It sounded like there was something hammering on the roof of the car!

Clump-clump. Clump-clump.

There it was again! It sounded like there was someone on the roof of the car! But maybe, she thought, it was just a low hanging branch that had fallen, or something. She wasn't sure. She didn't know anything about the woods, and it seemed like Mark had been gone for ages, and she was really scared. Every thump against the roof sent lightning bolts of terror shooting through her heart. She started to slump down in her seat.

Clump-clump. Clump-clump. Clump-clump.

"Mark! Mark! Oh, Mark, where are you?"

Every hammering thump on the roof made her more frenzied with terror, and she slumped down in the passenger seat floor, shivering in terror, until finally she became so exhausted from fear she passed out, still hearing the weird clump-clump sound as she faded into unconsciousness.

As Maddy opened her eyes, she realized the sun was coming up. Outside, she could see flashing lights. A police car! She climbed up into her seat and opened the car door, slowly and wearily.

"Come with me, miss! No, just get out of the car slowly. DON'T LOOK BEHIND YOU."

As the Sheriff was speaking another cop car pulled up, and an ambulance. Maddy thought, for a minute that the ambulance was for her. A lady ambulance attendant approached her, put a blanket around her shoulders, and helped her out of the car. Maddy felt pretty groggy from her all-night ordeal of terror.

"Come with me. Don't look behind you," said the lady ambulance attendant.

Suddenly, Maddy heard the strange thumping sound again as she walked through the tall grasses to the ambulance. She inadvertently glanced over her shoulder, and her eyes popped open. She swung around, out of the arms of the lady ambulance attendant, and the blanket on her shoulders fell to the grass.

She couldn't believe what she was looking at.

She screamed.

And screamed.

And screamed.

She finally knew what that strange sound was. It was the thump of a pair of hiking boots on the roof of the car. They were being worn by a body, hanging from the neck by a noose. The noose was wrapped around the slack, dead face of a handsome young man that she had been with only a few short hours before. It looked like he had been involved in a struggle. If so, it had been short-lived.

It was Mark.

13

Dancing with the Devil

It was a slow night at the club, but Lieutenant Prescott Purvis sauntered in, pulled off his cap, and sat down, grateful to be away from duty for a little while. He often thought it would be a much better war if a man could only get a little more rest and relaxation once in a while.

It was as hot as Hades outside, and the muddy streets outside were a nightmare to have to slosh through. Also, the mosquitoes here were fearsome; he thought he probably had a hundred bites all up and down his body, but he was too tired at the end of the day to count. The barkeep didn't speak much English, but for what Lieutenant Purvis needed, he didn't have to.

Purvis took the bottle and held it up to his lips. Even the beer here was lousy. Just as bad as the weather and the bugs. He sighed to himself, took a sip, and laid the bottle down. It was a nightmare alright: The place was nothing but rain, jungle, heat, bugs, and locals that didn't want you around. Oh well, he knew what he was in for when he signed up, he figured.

A few soldiers sauntered in looking bored. Above him, a ceiling fan chugged away quietly, not doing anything to cool down the sweltering heat that left you sweating like a pig with every move you made. He heard a fly buzz past his ear, but he was too tired to lift a finger to slap it away.

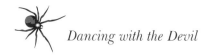

The place was dark and hot, just like the entire island. And pretty lonely, too, here in the backwaters of the South Pacific.

He lit a cigarette, sending curls of blue smoke down the length of the bar. Oh boy, another night, and then he would be back at the barracks, and then it wouldn't be long before he was back on duty, shuffling papers for the war effort. It wasn't a glamour job, and it sure wasn't going to make him a war hero in anybody's eyes. What kind of stories would he have to tell the kids, assuming he ever had any? That he fought the Japanese by filing reports and sitting behind a desk?

He sighed. The barkeep was washing glasses and drying them with an old rag. Lieutenant Purvis lifted his bottle to his mouth, drank, and watched a dying fly crawl across a puddle of spilled beer on the counter. Above him, the ceiling fan sent crazy shadows swinging across the bar, as a few tired soldiers played cards.

Suddenly, the door swung open, and a woman in a bright red dress sauntered in. Every pair of eyes in the bar suddenly shot up. She was the most beautiful thing anyone had ever seen around these parts. A classy dame; she looked like she had just stepped out of a Hollywood picture.

She had a huge coif of raven dark hair, and a red bow tied around it; the fabulous dress looked like it cost a million dollars. Lieutenant Purvis suddenly felt his head shoot up. He momentarily forgot his tiredness and his boredom.

She was carrying a little black handbag, and she had beautiful eyes and eyelashes that seemed a mile long. Her lips were done up pretty impressively, too. She didn't look like she belonged around here, at all.

Before Purvis knew it, the woman had sidled up to the bar, said something to the barkeep in his native language, and then sat right beside him.

"Well, hello there, soldier. What's your name?"

She had a voice that was soft and heavy at the same time, and maybe a little sassy. Like she was maybe a voice teacher for glamorous actresses. Lieutenant Purvis swallowed hard. Classy dames like this always made him feel nervous.

"Purvis, M'am. Lieutenant Purvis. Pleased to meet you."

The woman smiled. She was so beautiful he felt like a skinny, ugly farm boy from Idaho compared to her. Which, of course, was exactly what he was.

"Well, pleased to meet you, too, Lieutenant. My name is Lilith. Lilith Lucifer."

She put out on delicate hand, with long black nails, and he took it. He noticed she was wearing a weird ring with a strange symbol like a star on it. He kissed her hand, and the barkeep brought her a drink.

"My usual," she said, lifting the glass and draining it in one gulp. One of the soldiers in the back plunked some change into the beat up old jukebox, and suddenly some jazz music come floating across the bar.

"Hey," she said, slowly, looking at him with her icy green eyes, "do you wanna dance?"

He swallowed hard again. She was so beautiful! He had never seen a woman like her before. What was she doing here on the island? He felt like a gawky, clumsy, ugly jerk, but he said, "Yeah, sure. I'd like that."

He got up from the bar stool, and put his arms around her. He was never very good at slow dancing, but he did his best. He was just hypnotized by staring into those strange, green eyes. And, man, could she really dance!

They danced slowly and easily, and the music swelled, as some of the soldiers at the card table whistled and made little comments he didn't much care for. Oh well, he was mesmerized by her incredible eyes; just staring into them made him feel young and alive.

Of course, her hands were awfully cold. He thought that that was odd, considering the whole place was sweltering, but he didn't say anything about it. Also, she was wearing some kind of strange perfume. He had never smelled any scent like it before. It smelled like bitter almonds.

"What...what's that perfume you're wearing called?"

"Cyanide."

"Oh." He didn't know much about perfumes, and he thought that that sounded like a funny name.

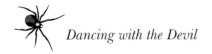

Her face was so gorgeous, her eyes so hypnotic, that the dance seemed to go on forever. Her heavy black heels clacked against the wooden floor of the bar, and he found it a little annoying. But the dance was so wonderful he wanted it to go on forever.

Suddenly, one of the soldiers at the card table in the back hissed, and said, "Geez louise! Boys, get a load of those!"

Lieutenant Purvis turned around, ready to yell at the drunken oaf, and was surprised to find the whole table of soldiers out of their chairs in shock. The one that had yelled out in surprise was pointing at the feet of his dancing partner, and his eyes were as big as twin moons.

Purvis looked down at the shiny black shoes of lovely Lilith Lucifer. He suddenly felt his heart flutter in shock. Now he understood why her shoes had been making so much noise on the barroom floor while they danced.

The barkeep dropped a glass, yelled in his native tongue, and crossed himself.

Purvis couldn't believe what he was seeing. Those shiny black shoes were not shoes at all.

They weren't even feet.

They were a pair of black, cloven *hooves*.

His eyes shot up to Lilith's beautiful face. Except, it wasn't so beautiful anymore. Now it was growing more hideous as he stared at it in disbelief. It grew too white, and the eyes grew black and menacing, and the teeth seemed to grow into horrid fangs while the lips curled back in maniacal laughter. The red bow in her thick black hair suddenly became a pair of glowing horns, and her laughter was the cruelest laughter he had ever heard. It sounded like ice chipping and cracking.

She vanished, suddenly disappearing in a cloud of smelly smoke. Lieutenant Purvis reeled backward, gagging on the horrible smell of rotten eggs. He could still hear the ringing echo of her icy laughter in his ears, as he came to the shocking conclusion that he had been DANCING WITH THE DEVIL!

14

Ghost Mom

Father Berringer was kneeling in his study, lost in fervent prayer, when a knock sounded at the door. He was surprised for a moment, as it was very late and rain was pattering against the windows. He got up with a sigh, wondering if he should answer it (it was, after all, a very dangerous neighborhood, and they had had a series of home-invasions lately), then decided that he should at least see who it was. After all, it might be one of his parishioners in serious need.

He got up and went to the door, peering out through the spy hole before asking, in a wary voice, "Who is it?"

"Father Berringer, I need to speak with you. It's..."

But he didn't catch the last name. Outside, a small, white-haired old woman was standing shivering in the cold. She didn't seem as if she meant any harm, so he slowly undid the deadbolt and opened the door.

The woman came into the room, looking grateful. She said, "Father Berringer, I am so sorry to interrupt you this late in the evening, but I have something I need to discuss with you. Something important."

Still a little taken aback, he stuttered for a moment, feeling foolish, and then asked, "Excuse me, Ma'm, but are you one of my flock? You...seem familiar. Have we met before?"

The woman, who was awfully pale he suddenly realized, said, "I was a parishioner long ago. I've moved on to another place…Anyway, what I wanted to speak to you about was my son, Father. My son…"

The woman trailed off. Father Berrigan realized, all of a sudden, how strange and far away her gaze was. She looked as if she was not altogether well in the head, and Father Berrigan wondered for a moment if he shouldn't perhaps contact the mental health authorities. But, before he would do that, he would make her sit down and at least have a cup of tea.

"Excuse me…" He looked at her, obviously waiting for her to give him her name.

"Barbara. My name is Barbara Bentley."

"Yes, Barbara. My, that name sounds familiar. Well, Barbara, I seem to have forgotten my manners. Will you please sit down? Can I get you a cup of tea? You look chilled to the bone."

The woman took a seat, but said, "I can't really stay very long. I must be moving on. And I never drink…tea. Father, I have something very special to ask of you. I need you to go to my son. He's been having a horrible time of it lately, and he's been drinking very heavily. He lost his job you see…"

Father Berrigan looked down at the floor rather sadly. He had heard the same story all week: layoffs, foreclosures, people out of work and needing charity or a place to stay.

"Yes," he sighed, sadly. "These are very trying times."

"Yes, indeed," she said, as if she wasn't really that interested in talking about the times, and how trying they may or may not be. She continued: "Well, I need you to go and see my son, Joe. Father, his heart is bad, and he's not going to make it. I need you to go to Joe, and I need you to administer the sacraments to him. He's going to be called home soon, and he won't have a priest near him when he goes. Which will be late tomorrow night."

Father Berrigan felt his mouth fall open. He had never before been asked to do such a thing, and he wasn't sure if he had even understood correctly what she had just said. He asked, "Excuse me? Is this some sort of a prank?"

The woman seemed offended for a moment, and then said, "Oh no Father, I promise you, this is serious. Very, very serious. As serious as it gets. Joe has always been a good Catholic, even

if he has been having personal trouble as of late. It would be horrible if he should die without having the sacraments."

Father Berrigan said, "Oh, yes, of course. Well, I'll make sure and go and see him."

The woman looked a little troubled now.

"Oh, you must go as soon as you can tonight. There isn't much time left. And I'm afraid he won't come to see you. He's gotten awfully bitter, and he is drinking pretty heavily now."

Father Berrigan felt his eyes fall to the carpet. He hadn't wanted to leave the house this evening, and it was raining. It seemed the perfect night to curl up in front of the fireplace in his study. He didn't wish to go out visiting at all really, but the woman seemed so sincere, he didn't see how he could refuse her.

"Okay," he said, "I'll get my things together and go see him."

At that the woman seemed to be overjoyed, and said, "Oh, thank you Father Berrigan! Thank you! Thank you! Why, this is the nicest thing anyone has ever done for me and Joe."

Father Berrigan got up, said, "Do you want to take your car, or mine?"

The woman suddenly looked confused, and said, "Why, no, I couldn't do that. I'm not…going to be able to go with you, Father. But here's the address."

And she handed him a small, yellowed piece of paper with an address scrawled on it. He said, a little surprised, "You mean, you're not coming with me?"

"Oh, no. I…I can't. I just can't, although I sure would like to, Father. It's a lot to explain. Just go to that address, and knock. He'll be at home. As for me, I have to go now. But I thank you from the bottom of my heart. And God bless you, Father Berrigan. I mean it, really. God bless you."

And with that the woman turned and walked across the living room, and out the door.

He suddenly went to the door just as she shut it. He opened it up…and she was gone. How had she disappeared so fast? *Weird*, he thought. He shivered a little, wondering where she had parked.

Father Berrigan stood there for awhile, feeling puzzled. What on earth was all this about, really? He didn't know.

Probably just some lonely old woman's crazy vision. For a moment he felt like tearing the address up and going up to bed, but he knew, deep inside, that that would be wrong. He grabbed his coat and hat, and a little case in which he carried his things. Then, he went out, making sure to click off all the lights in the house. Just his luck, it was still raining.

He drove out to a part of town that gave him the real creeps.

It was a rundown section of the city, with sprawling industrial parks and factories, and crumbling buildings, and stores that had bars on the windows, and houses that looked like they had been burned out. Creepy hoods walked in the shadows, and graffiti was spray painted all over the place. Foul words.

Father Berrigan shuddered. He didn't really want to park his car in this bad area, but he knew he had little choice. He finally found the building.

It was a crumbling apartment house that looked as bad as everything else around there. In the doorway a homeless man was standing, trying for some shelter beneath the tin awning. He looked at the slip of paper the old woman had given him before she did her weird vanishing act. Joe lived in 22B. He got out, making sure to lock his doors.

He went into the place, past the old wino in the doorway, and found himself at the bottom of the stairs. Great.

He trudged up, noting the streaks of crayon and other graffiti on the wall, the general filthy look of the place. It smelled bad, too. It smelled greasy and moldy, and stale with the smell of cigarette smoke and garbage. He passed a door where he could hear a child screaming as the parents yelled at each other. He could hear what sounded like objects being thrown around.

This is the sort of place, he thought, you wonder if you are going to make it out of in one piece.

He found 22B, and knocked. He waited. He knocked louder.

Suddenly, he could hear someone yell, hoarsely, and rumble around behind the door.

The door was suddenly opened. The man who opened it started to utter a curse before he saw who was standing there.

"Father? What...what can I do for you?"

The man seemed really confused. He had on a filthy t-shirt, his hair was a mess, his eyes were bloodshot and had dark circles underneath them, and he needed a shave. He didn't smell like roses, either.

"Sorry to disturb you, Joe. Your mother paid me a visit tonight. Said I should come over and administer the sacraments to you. Said she had a vision or something..." Father Berrigan trailed off, not wanting to tell Joe that his mother had actually said that Joe was going to die soon. He figured you just didn't tell someone something like that.

"My...mother? Father, are you sure? Wait, I've forgotten my manners. C'mon in."

Father Berrigan stepped through the door. The place was a mess, with pizza delivery boxes, used TV dinner trays, and candy wrappers spilling out of wastebaskets and littering the floor and the cracked coffee table. There were also a lot of empty beer and liquor bottles, overflowing ashtrays, and a terrible smell coming from the kitchen. Father Berrigan wrinkled his nose, and said, "Your mother said you've hit some hard times, Joe. She seemed really worried."

Joe sat down, his head hanging down in confusion, and said, "Father, are you sure it was my mother? Wait, what's your name Father?"

"Berrigan. I'm Father Berrigan. Yes, she said she was your mother. Said you hadn't been to church in a long time. Said she thought you had lost your faith."

Joe suddenly ran his fingers through his dirty head and sighed, saying, "Geez, Father. I don't know what to say. I mean, I'm not calling you a liar or anything but...Are you certain she told you she was my mother?"

Father Berrigan suddenly felt irritated. He said, "Yes. She said she was your mother. Barbara Bentley. Said I need to come here immediately and administer the sacraments. So here I am. You are Joe Bentley, right?"

The man suddenly blow air out of his mouth in a gusty sigh, and nodded, "Oh, I'm Joe Bentley alright. I appreciate you coming Father Berrigan. But, you'll pardon me if I'm really confused about all this. You see, what you've just told me is impossible. Just…impossible."

Father Berrigan frowned. He said, "Impossible, you say. Why?"

Joe opened his mouth, started to speak, and then found he couldn't. He then said, his voice trembling a little, "Well, Father, you said that my mother visited you tonight, and told you to come see me. Well, Father, that's just impossible because my mother is dead."

Father Berrigan felt his moth drop open. His hands began to tremble, and he suddenly felt very cold all over. He started to stutter out a few words, but found he just couldn't say anything.

"She's been dead for nine months. Look. Her picture is right over there on the wall."

Father Berrigan walked over to the wall on trembling legs, and looked at the photo. He felt the icy stab of fear grip his heart. It was the woman he had talked with only a few hours ago.

He turned to Joe, swallowed hard, said, "Well…I'm here. She wanted me to come here for a reason. Are you ready Joe?"

Joe said he was, and Father Berrigan administered the sacraments.

Later, he went around the corner to buy some beer before the liquor store closed. Man, he needed a drink, he thought. Tonight had been just too…creepy. Father Berrigan had left after a promise from Joe that he would come to Mass as soon as possible. Well, he decided that he sure enough would keep that promise.

He opened the door of the ugly, weathered liquor store and walked in. He went down the aisle, grabbed a case of beer, and hefted it over to the counter. He set it down, and the sleepy-looking cashier began to ring him up as Joe reached for his wallet.

Suddenly, he felt a stabbing pain in his chest. He groaned, grabbing his heart, and dropped to the dirty floor.

The cashier said, "Mister? Hey man, don't you die here, man!"

The cashier started to dial an ambulance, but it was too late.

Joe was gone.

When Father Berrigan read about it in the newspaper the next day, he was chilled to the bone. Then he closed the paper, sat back, heaved a gusty sigh, and smiled. Poor Joe. He had had a tough time of it in life, and now he was gone.

Then Father Berrigan thought better of it. He remembered how much Joe had loved his mother. At last, he thought, partly thanks to his own efforts, they were together again. This time, forever.

15

Aren't You Glad You Didn't Turn on the Light?

Lola and her friend Bridget had been sharing a dorm room all year, and Bridget was starting, frankly, to get on Lola's nerves. It wasn't just the weird hours that Bridget kept, it was nearly everything about her: her weird music, her creepy friends, and the way she did her hair up, in a big, messy coif, like the Bride of Frankenstein. Also, Bridget was really strange. She was always staring off into space, writing macabre poetry, and talking about, "like, how beautiful things were when they decayed."

Ugh. Lola wasn't sure how much more she could take, but since the semester was almost over, she planned to go to her RA and ask if she could get a transfer. Their study habits were so different, Lola was having a hard time keeping up on her work, and she rarely got a good night's sleep because Bridget thrashed and cried out when she was sleeping. She said the strangest things in her sleep! Stuff that really freaked Lola out.

However, she figured she should be able to stand it for just a few more weeks. After all, she had tolerated it so far, and nothing really bad had happened.

It was late during Finals Week when she first met Matt McGruder. He was tall, handsome, and, like totally the cutest guy she had ever met in her entire life. She had just met him coming out of one of his finals, rubbing his chin, which had a few days worth of beard growth on it. He had obviously been up all night, studying.

"Hey there," she said, not entirely sure why she felt so compelled to talk to him. "You look like you've really been cramming!"

He looked up at her with bleary eyes.

"Yeah, I haven't gotten much sleep lately. Man, that test sure was real pain. Dr. Moskalew has to be one of the toughest profs on the faculty."

Feeling a little more brave, she suddenly thrust out her hand, said, "Hi! I'm Lola. I think I've seen you around a couple times this semester. Never got a chance to talk to you before."

He suddenly smiled, and his smile was gorgeous, too.

"Oh yeah. Well, same here. I'm Matt. Say, what are you doing right now. Got a final?"

Her heart soared all of a sudden with excitement, and she said, innocently enough, "No, I'm free for the rest of the day. Why?"

He looked a little shy for a moment, and then said, "Would you like to go get a cup of coffee with me, Lola? I could use the company and the conversation."

She laughed a little nervously. Inside, her heart was jumping up and down with butterflies, but she said, "Sure! I'd love to."

That had been three days ago, and so far they had been out every day together. It was turning into a real whirlwind romance. The only problem was when Matt came back to her dorm room and Bridget was there. Bridget was sullen and quiet and as weird as usual, with her black eye make-up and her strange t-shirts that had skulls all over them. Also, she would often watch gory old horror movies with the sound turned down and gothic rock music turned up. A real space cadet. (But Lola also knew that Bridget was a Straight *A* student, and was a lot smarter than her, even if she was so cockamamie weird.)

Matt seemed interested in Bridget, and even tried to make small talk with her. But Bridget just brushed him off. The kind of guys Bridget liked were not jockey guys that looked like football players, but really skinny guys with lots of pierced body parts and weird haircuts. They usually smoked clove cigarettes and dressed all in black. Lola thought they were all losers, but she always kept her mouth shut around them.

Of course, since her and Bridget would be parting ways soon, it didn't really matter if her and Matt got along. The rest of Finals Week was the most fun that Lola had had since she had been at college (it was still only her sophomore year), and she thanked her lucky stars that she had had the good fortune to finally run into Matt at the right place, at the right time, and had had the courage to introduce herself, finally.

They went out to a nice dinner at a fancy Italian place, and had so much fun that Lola almost forgot that her most important final was coming up that Friday. It was in Dr. Stern's Psychology class, and was a real monster even for a lower-level course. She knew that she would have to pry herself free from Matt all night Thursday, and the idea alone made her feel sort of gloomy.

She was already head-over-heels in love, she thought.

She called him and told him: "Matt, I really can't do anything tonight. I'm cramming for Dr. Stern's psych test tomorrow, and I need to read, like, all night. The test is at seven o'clock in the morning…so, I'm gonna be pulling an all-nighter."

"Aw, that's too bad, babe. Say, can I at least drop by and say hi?"

She thought for a moment.

"I'll probably be in the library until it closes, and then the study lounge. I'm not sure what time I'm gonna be back. Late. Really late. As late as you can imagine. So, probably I won't be there all night. Unless I just get so tired I pass out, or something."

Matt sounded a little disappointed, but said, "Hey, I understand! Just give me a call Friday night and let me know how things went, and we'll make plans for this weekend. Okay?"

"Okay," she said, thankfully. He was turning out to be the best boyfriend in the world. The most understanding and caring, she thought, she had ever dated.

Wow.

She bundled her books together with a sigh, headed out the door of her room, leaving Bridget (who she sometimes thought looked a lot like that actress Winona Ryder when she starred in that old movie *Beetlejuice*) in front of one of her vampire movies, listening to Bauhaus with her headphones on. She headed out the door and down the hall, to the library, which looked like a huge, red, modern fortress and was the biggest building on campus.

She hated libraries. They always gave her the creeps.

She found the study room that she had reserved especially for herself, plunked her book bag down on the table, didn't like the silence one little bit (it was so quiet in the library you could hear a pin drop) and got out her books and folders and pens and notepads. She cracked the book, determined to read through every chapter, even if just skimming the info, and compare it to the notes she had taken in class. After an hour, she yawned.

Hours went by. She could feel her legs getting cramped, and she got up to get herself a drink of water. On the way, she passed the checkout desk and glanced up at the clock. It was time to go and get something in one of the student eateries, and so she went back upstairs, gathered up her belongings, and walked across campus, which was really beautiful with the sun setting but which was pretty empty with students having already left for break after completing their finals.

She got herself a big meal at the student buffet, and didn't realize how hungry she was until she started eating. She dug in, not liking the fact that she would soon have to return to the little study room at the library for more work.

After another few hours, when she had made her way through a lot of the material, the lights went out in the library. She looked up for a minute, startled, and then realized that this was what they did right before they closed, to let students know they had fifteen minutes to gather their things, check out whatever needed checking out, and get out. She yawned, stretched, knew she should probably go downstairs to the 24-hour computer lab and continue studying all night. Then she realized just how sleepy she was.

Her vision was blurry and her eyes were sore. She felt like she could hardly hold her head up any longer. Why hadn't she studied harder this week? She knew Dr. Stern's test would be really tough. She had only herself to blame if she got a lousy grade.

She then reminded herself that she had gotten perfectly acceptable grades so far, and that she knew most of the material anyway, if not every little bit of it. Maybe she was being too hard on herself. At any rate, if she went downstairs and studied all night, she might very well pass out in the computer lab, and sleep through the test at one of the cubicles. No one would bother to wake her up. She wasn't their responsibility.

So she made the decision to trudge across the quad back to her dorm room, and turn in for a few hours. That way, she figured, she would be mentally fresh when it came time to take the test in the morning. She would make sure to set her alarm. She would probably end up acing the test, and then she would come home and take a nap. After that, Friday night would belong to her and Matt. Probably they would go get a pizza and see a movie, she thought, smiling to herself.

She walked across the quad, which was just about empty and which was kind of spooky this late. Her residence hall was just down the walk, but the rustle of dead leaves in the breeze made her feel nervous. They sounded like someone was crunching them as they followed her across the pavement toward her dorm, and she jumped nervously a time or two, in spite of herself.

She let herself in with her student ID. The commissary was closed, and the halls were empty, although she could hear the occasional TV. It was supposed to be "quiet hours" all during Finals Week, but a few people obviously couldn't obey the rules. Also, she thought she heard some young guys cutting up and probably drinking behind another door as she passed by. Oh well, the extra noise made her feel a little less creepy.

She finally got to her own room door, and all was quiet inside. It was also pitch dark (Bridget had insisted on black curtains and always liked it pitch dark), and Lola, who wore glasses and was near-sighted, had to let her eyes adjust a bit before she could make her way to her bed, throw down her book bag, get undressed, and collapse. She decided not to turn on the lights, because she didn't want to disturb Bridget, who seemed to be sleeping peacefully for once.

She sighed as she slid between the cool sheets. Ah! It felt like heaven!

Wait? What was that noise?

She could have sworn she heard something rustling in the darkness. And it sounded like there was breathing. Heavy breathing.

At first, she wondered if her nerves might just be getting to her. Maybe she had been studying too hard, and the stress was getting to her or something. She didn't know. All of a sudden, she felt scared.

Then she felt really afraid. She could barely make out the outline of someone sitting in a big comfortable chair near the door. She suddenly felt her heart twinge, and she started to pull the covers away.

"Boo!" said a familiar voice in a hoarse whisper.

Her heart almost skipped a beat before she realized who it was.

"Oh Matt, it's you!" She said, feeling a huge amount of relief well up in her. "What are you doing here?"

The figure got up from the chair and tip-toed quietly over to her bedside, leaned down, and whispered, "I came over just as your weird roommate was getting ready for bed. Sheesh! She sure is some piece of work, isn't she? I just couldn't stand not seeing you today, so I asked her if I could wait around until you got back. She said that it was cool, that she had some new meds from her doctor that were to help her sleep."

Bridget Breedlove was off in a sleepy-bye land that looked like something out of a Tim Burton movie.

She was dressed a little like the Bride of Frankenstein, and she was walking up a hill that came to a weird, craggy point in the distance. It was dark, and the trees looked like gnarled and crooked fingers rising up to the sky. At the top of the weird, craggy peak was an old house straight out of a haunted storybook. Inside, she knew her true love (who looked an awful lot like Johnny Depp in the movie *Edward Scissorhands*) was waiting for her to come and rescue him from the clutches of an evil scientist who had trapped him for the purposes of doing weird experiments on him because he was an alien, or vampire, or something strange and thrilling that she couldn't quite recall later, after she had woken up.

She hurried up the darkened path, past the old, crooked fingered trees, and onto the rickety front porch. The doorway of the strange house was designed to look as if a skeleton with long arms and legs was built into the frame. She opened the creaky old thing, and suddenly became choked up with dust in the darkness.

Inside, the whole house seemed bigger, and like it might have been designed for the set of an old Universal horror movie. There were glowing candelabras, huge cobwebs, an uneven stone floor, and a staircase that wound up into the darkness. It had a heavy red carpet on it the color of blood. There was a huge stone fireplace with a mantle and bizarre objects that looked hideous and ancient resting atop it. There were all sorts of creepy old paintings on the wall, of ancient people whose eyes seemed to follow you as you went past them. There was even a suit of armor.

She walked inside, Faintly, she could hear someone playing the organ somewhere. She thought it might be that silly thing by Bach that seemed to be on every Halloween record she had ever owned (and she had owned a bunch), but then it started veering off into wild, strange directions and seemed to totally become random and weird. She thought she could also hear something that sounded like a ghostly choir, but she wasn't sure.

She walked into the creepy old house slowly, and then a little faster as the door slammed by itself behind her. She tuned, gulped, and then started to inch her way across the dirty, uneven floor, listening to the squeak of a few huge rats in the corner. Good thing she couldn't see them; she hated rats.

But, she loved spiders! And the web that stretched across the staircase had a lovely, large tarantula crawling through it, with yellow rings around its hairy legs. Really lovely. She wanted to reach out and pet that spider, but when she tried, her hand just passed through it, as if she were a ghost.

She slowly climbed the stairs, her shadow growing long in the dim light from the flickering candles, until she came to the first floor landing. There were a number of dark, heavy doors on either side of the hall, and she slowly crept down until she came to one where she thought she could see a light creep out from underneath. She put her ear to the door. She could hear a faint sobbing.

She reached into her cloak and suddenly was amazed to find a key hidden in the folds. She pulled it out, noting that it looked like an old-fashioned skeleton key, and inserted it into the lock, hearing the lock rattle and clatter as she twisted the key around. She pushed open the door, which groaned and creaked. She realized the weeping had stopped.

Inside, by the light of a flickering torch, she saw the most beautiful guy she had ever seen in her life, like a mixture of Johnny Depp and Peter Murphy from Bauhaus rolled into one. He looked so sad and lonely, and then his face seemed to brighten and the tears of joy began to fall as she raced forward into his arms.

But then a horrible thing happened! She felt an electric tingling all over her body, and she found she couldn't come close to falling into the arms of her sweet, dark prince because of a magic force field that surrounded him on all sides. It made an electrical static sound every time she tried to come close to him, and it gave her an electric shock that almost knocked her off her feet. They both stood there looking at each other for a moment, their arms stretched toward each other helplessly when, all of a sudden the door (which had somehow become shut again), suddenly flew open, revealing the image of a gnarled old man that she knew was an evil sorcerer. He was tall and ugly, and wore a huge hooded cape, and had long gnarled black fingers that looked like tree branches. What's more, he seemed to float across the floor like he was on roller skates, and a high, piercing scream erupted from him as he dove toward her!

Bridget sat up groggily in bed, her eyes bleary, nearly blind from the darkness. Her head was swimming from the powerful medication her therapist had given her (her therapist had told her it would help her sleep better), and she wasn't sure if she was awake or dreaming. It looked like her preppy, snobby roommate, the dumb blonde with the creepy new boyfriend, was thrashing around in the dark. Probably having a nightmare. Then it looked like there was maybe someone lying in bed with her. But it was so dark, and Bridget was so tired and drugged she couldn't tell. She reached over to turn on the nightstand light, but then thought it too far and too much effort. She collapsed on her front, falling back to sleep, the last thought on her mind as she went back to dreamland and the haunted castle being, *Oh yeah, Matt came over and wanted to hang out and wait for her. It must just be those two making out or something. Wow, Lola isn't so squeaky clean as she tries to make out! Did Lola really scream, or was it just part of my dream?*

Bridget traveled back to the strange peaked hill, only this time she was a female superhero, intent on saving her Prince Charming from the dark house and living "happily ever after."

The first few warm rays of the sun peeping through the blinds caused Bridget to slowly open her bleary eyes. Man, that had been a night of wild dreams! She lay in bed on her back as her eyes adjusted to the gloomy natural light that was flooding into the room. Suddenly she noticed something strange on the ceiling.

Looked like someone had painted a weird pattern on the ceiling while she was asleep. In droplets of bloody red.

She suddenly sat up, remembering what she had seen last night when she had momentarily woken up from her strange and wonderful dreams. Her eyes traveled over to her roommate's bed. Suddenly, she felt a scream jump up and catch in her throat.

Being the kind of person she was though, her shock was short-lived. She got up from her bed and walked over to her roommate's bed, looking down at the bloody, gory mess that was splattered all over the bed sheets. Of course, she knew immediately who did this. Written on the wall over the bed were the words:

Aren't you glad you didn't turn on the light?

In dripping, bloody letters. Suddenly, she realized that if she just stood there calmly and then went and called the police, she would end up the prime suspect herself! And, of course, it must have been Lola's creepy new boyfriend.

All of a sudden, she let out an earsplitting scream, ran out the door and down the hall, shouting "Murder!" at the top of her lungs, and pulling the fire alarm. She later thought that that might have been going too far, but even if it was, it had the desired effect of bringing everyone out into the hallway. Shortly, screams began to be heard all around the residence hall, and the cops came screeching up with their sirens screaming and their lights flashing.

Matt, incidentally, was found innocent. He claimed to have stayed for a few minutes, then left. He said Lola followed him to the door, and that was the last time he saw her alive. DNA evidence seemed to support his claims, and he was acquitted. To this day, the murder of Lola Lana Leman remains officially "unsolved."

As for Bridget Breedlove, she went on to write a best-selling series of vampire novels, after months of intense psychotherapy and appearances on a few big-time television talk shows. She made millions of dollars, married a Hollywood star that looked a little too much like Johnny Depp, and lived to a ripe old age in a strange dark house perched atop a craggy hill.

16

The Mummy

Ben and Sherry were on their first date, and it was turning out to be a humdinger. They had driven up to the Flag Island Amusement Park, and had spent the entire day and more money than they could possibly afford riding the rides and playing silly games. Ben won Sherry a stuffed animal with the Flag Island logo on it, and they rode a roller coaster that made Sherry so sick she nearly puked up the hot dogs and French fries they had eaten earlier.

The place was great, they decided, and as they walked down the boardwalk in front of a row of booths. They could hear old-fashioned organ music come piping out of one of the rides up ahead.

"Oh Ben," said Sherry. "Everything is perfect. I just love amusement parks!"

He nodded his head in agreement. It was all perfect: the sights and smells, the weird assortment of animals and people, the hanging garden exhibit, the bright lights and the rides, and the sound of the kids crying over spilt pop and melting ice cream cones. The sun was already dipping low on the horizon, and great clouds of dust had sprung up—the whole thing was just too good to be true.

"Yes," said Ben. "You're right. For once, I think we made the perfect choice in coming here. What a great place this is. Why, it makes me feel like a kid all over again!"

Ben suddenly realized where the music was coming from. It was up ahead, and across the dusty midway. It was coming from the Spook House.

"Oh look," said Ben, pointing his finger. "It's the one place we haven't been yet. I love horror stuff! C'mon! We still have some tokens left, I think."

Sherry hesitated. She never liked to be scared the way Ben did. It gave her the willies, and she knew some of those Spook House places weren't built too well. It could be dangerous.

"Are you sure?" she said.

He could tell she didn't want to go, but he was not to be talked out of it. "C'mon. It's perfectly safe. It's just a ride. This place is the safest place on earth! What could possibly go wrong?"

He started on ahead a little bit, and though he tried, he couldn't keep that little-boy enthusiasm from glowing brightly on his face. And she followed him. He could tell that she didn't really feel like walking through the Spook House right now. She probably felt like sitting out by the lake and watching the fireworks display. But he knew that she wanted to make him happy, too. And she knew he lived for this kind of stuff.

Ben stood out in front of the place for a minute, taking it all in. It was just like one of those old movie sets they used in westerns decades ago. The whole front of the place was false, hammered together to look like something from an old episode of the Addams Family, with mannequins dressed to look like witches and ghosts and Frankenstein's monster peeping out of nooks and crannies and from fake balconies. An immense fat woman (who seemed to be some sort of mechanical puppet) sat on the roof, laughing and laughing, while the creepy organ music poured out of hidden speakers in the old place.

Ben hammered up the stairs, with Sherry not far behind him. At the doorway, a bored carnie with heaving muscles and faded tattoos took their tokens and pushed a little buzzer on a panel in front of him. The ornate doors swung open to a recording of a shriek and then a sinister laugh, and then they just as quickly slammed behind.

"Well," said Ben, "it looks like we're the only ones in here right now."

"Yeah," said Sherry, nervously. "Pretty popular attraction, huh?"

There were neon green arrows pointing down the darkened halls. The walls, Ben noted, were full of huge paintings of leering devils,

graveyards, full moons, werewolves, and pictures of old movie actors like Bela Lugosi and Vincent Price. The sounds of the eerie organ music filled the halls, and every once in awhile a recording of a woman screaming or someone growling would echo through the passages. In a few corners lighted display cases held some pretty gruesome models: stuff like rotted zombies, and Halloween monster masks that were a little too real. In one case, there was even one of those electrical things that shot sparks like lightning bolts up and down.

"What do you call that thing?" Sherry asked.

Ben said, "I think they call it a 'Tesla Coil'. They have one in all those old movies."

They walked on, passing through a few different rooms made up to look like scenes from old horror movies. There was a mad scientist's lab with a grinning maniac of a wax dummy bending over a surgical table. The table was covered by a sheet, but there was clearly a body underneath. Suddenly, as they followed the neon green arrows and got closer to the table, the mechanical dummy beneath the sheet sprang upward with a recorded moan and groan.

Ben and Sherry jumped, startled at the sudden movement. Then they started laughing at themselves, realizing how they had been taken in by such a simple trick. The figure had the face of Frankenstein's monster from the old movie version.

"See, it looks just like Karloff!" said Ben, enthusiastically. Sherry was not so delighted. She noticed a bunch of fake wax arms with bloody stumps in a basket in the corner.

They moved on, although Ben probably could have stayed in one spot forever looking everything over and daydreaming. It was a little like being in one of his favorite old moves, for real.

They followed the green, glowing arrows down another cramped hall and into the next room, which looked like a scene straight out of Victorian England. The floor was like fake cobblestones, and there were gas lamps and dark windows, and a fog machine started. Everything looked dirty and a hundred years old, and really dark.

Suddenly, they noticed what looked like a woman lying on the ground in a pool of blood. They walked up to her.

It was another wax dummy, but it was a gory mess. Whoever did this particular display did a great job.

"Man," said Ben, "it all looks so real! I can't believe it! This is, like, the coolest place in the whole park!"

"Yeah, sure. Whatever you say." Sherry wasn't enjoying it nearly as much as Ben was, but, then, she wasn't the huge horror and sci-fi buff that he was, either. He loved comic books, horror flicks, science fiction, and all that other crap that she didn't have much enthusiasm for. He was like a big kid in a place like this.

"Hey, what's that noise?"

They suddenly heard a pair of what sounded like squeaky wheels or tracks, and a dark figure flew out at them from a nearby hallway that was made to look like an alley.

They both shrieked and flew back, and the tall image of the man in the cloak and top hat came a foot or two away from hem, raising one skinny arm above his head. In that arm was a bloody knife.

It was another robot. It was obviously on some kind of wheels or tracks, because as soon as it waved its knife arm up and down once or twice, it let out a sinister laugh, and then retracted back into the alleyway without even turning around.

Sherry felt her heart go leaping up into her throat. Fake or not, that had been scary. Real scary. Ben was also scared for a moment, but, then he started laughing. Sherry couldn't believe it. He actually seemed to enjoy being scared like this.

"I guess that was Jack the Ripper," he said, laughing nervously. "Man, this place is great. I could live here!"

"Yeah, well, you can move in by yourself if you want. Me, I'm for getting this creepy ride over with."

"Oh, come on! It's neat. It's fun to be scared." Ben was beaming. He always liked to prove how brave he was by being into this stuff. He suspected that Sherry thought it was because he was shorter than her, but she never said anything about it.

They followed the green arrows out of the Jack the Ripper exhibit, and past some windows that seemed to look onto an old-fashioned ballroom where ghostly figures in weird costumes seemed to be dancing the afterlife away. Ben stopped for a moment at the windows, but this didn't interest him as much. He had seen a TV special, and he knew exactly how this special effect was done. Also, he knew it wasn't very original. And it didn't really strike him as very spooky either.

"I know exactly how they do that. I saw it on the Historical Channel. You see--"

But she interrupted him. "Okay, Mr. Expert, let's get moving. We don't want to be here all night, do we?"

They followed the green arrows out of the ghostly ballroom display, and into a very narrow hall. And that's when the real fun began.

The floor was uneven, and springs underneath it made certain parts of it jump up all of a sudden, throwing them off balance.

"Be careful! Man, you'd think they'd have gotten rid of stuff like this, what with the threat of lawsuits from people maybe getting injured in here!" Ben was always thinking of stuff like this.

Sherry said, "Yeah, like what if someone really got hurt or something? Man, they could really clean up. But, I think it did say, painted somewhere on the wall back there that you 'Enter at your own risk!' Something like that."

He could see that she felt tired, all of a sudden, and just wanted to get the tour over with.

Suddenly, a horrible electric alarm went off, jolting them from their conversation.

Weird wires slapped against their ankles, probably, Ben thought, to represent rat tails.

A pair of giant green hands shot out from the darkness of the walls and grabbed at them—robot hands—but they came on so sudden that Sherry was starting to get fed up with all the sudden shocks and surprises. Would they ever get to the end of this Spook House attraction?

The sounds of screams and sinister laughter, and moans, and wolves howling filled the hallways, and a recorded voice came on and said, "It's getting…darker!" Then the voice erupted into a really grim laugh.

The next hall they came to was even smaller than the last one, and Sherry wondered out loud, "How does a really fat person manage to make it to the end of the ride?" It was also pitch dark now except for the arrows, and she put her hands to the edges of the walls, trailing her fingers across them.

Ben was in heaven.

Another loud alarm rang at the end of the hall, and a door slid up.

"Oh great!" said Sherry.

The next hallway was actually a revolving tunnel, and they had to get down on their hands and knees and crawl through. The tunnel was spinning at the time, so they both had to go in a kind of crawling, sideways motion to keep from spinning around on their hands and knees and falling on their backs. Now Sherry felt she had almost, finally, had enough of this particular "fun house." She was starting to feel sick, probably from the spinning tunnel she was crawling through. "I hope the next stop on this ride will be the EXIT…"

Of course, she thought to herself, *that is one of the strange things about this particular "spook house." I haven't seen one "chicken exit" the whole time we've been walking through here. Usually these places have plenty of emergency exits for people that can't handle it, or are too fat to get through the narrow hallways, or who suddenly find out that they're claustrophobic. Man, these people better make some quick changes to this place, or somebody, someday, is gonna sue their pants off.*

But she kept her thoughts to herself.

Finally, they made their way out of the spinning tunnel. Next up was a hall of mirrors, and Sherry actually sort of liked this, although getting through it was pretty tiring. She bumped into a few mirrors here and there, but it was amazing seeing both of their reflections shaped into tall, skinny, short, fat, and even accordion-shaped images. It was also neat seeing themselves reflected, a thousand times, down one length of mirrors, as if they existed in a thousand, million different places all at once. Weird.

"Wow," said Sherry. "You never told me how fat I was getting."

Ben liked the hall of mirrors. He said, "Look, it's like seeing yourself in other dimensions or something. Like a picture of an artist painting a picture, painting a picture, painting a picture, painting a picture…"

He trailed off. Finally, they were free of the mirrors, and faced with a weird new room. It seemed to contain only two doors. On each of the doors, a neon green question mark had been painted.

Doesn't this ever end? Sherry thought, exasperated, but she said, "I wonder which one is the right one?"

Ben said, 'I guess we'll just have to test it and find out."

He went, "Eeny meeny miny...mo!"

He leapt forward and opened the door to the left. Sherry swallowed, not liking this one bit. Apparently, the door didn't lead to the outside and the end of the ride, but to a set of stone steps that went down into a sort of basement.

"Okay," said Sherry. "Now I'm really confused."

"Oh," said Ben, "it's just part of the exhibit. Look; the green arrows are painted on each step."

Down the steps they went. It was very dark, so dark that they had trouble even seeing the neon green arrows, but finally they came to a sort of stone landing.

"Good evening!"

They both jumped out of their skin! There suddenly appeared a strange little man before them. He appeared almost as if he had jumped clean out of thin air, and they hadn't even had so much as a hint that he was standing in front of them before. He was scary! He drew out his "Good evening..." greeting long and slow, like it was a bunch of syllables long, and he had a weird accent that Sherry couldn't quite place.

He was obviously made up to look very ghoulish. He had a red hood on that fitted tight around his skull and joined at the neck, and flowed down to form a long red cape. His face was painted a ghastly green, and he had fake warts and arching eyebrows and piercing eyes. He was dressed completely in black from head to toe, and wore a long necklace that looked like a little white skull. On his shoulder, a rubber spider was perched menacingly.

"Greetings boys and ghouls! My name is Carter. You're darn lucky you picked the right door! If you had picked the wrong one...well, let's just say we wouldn't now be enjoying the pleasure of each other's company!"

Ben and Sherry looked at each other strangely. Neither one of them had been expecting anything like this.

Suddenly, somewhere in the darkness in back, something seemed to stumble around and growl. It sounded like it was carrying a heavy chain around with it.

"Boris! Boris, you be quiet back there. We have special guests. Yes, yes, I'll come back and feed you in a minute, Boris! You'll just have to hold your horses!"

Carter looked at them with a hideous gleam in is eyes.

"I'm sure he's extra hungry tonight!"

Ben gulped. Sherry felt faint. Carter continued.

"Since you both are such extra special guests, and had such a good time on our little tour, I've decided to let you in on the *real* main attraction around here! We don't let just anyone see it! It's reserved only for those special folks who feel themselves compelled to walk the pathways of darkness and face terror and wonder for the fun of it. You two are just such a pair. Aren't you?"

Carter leaned close to Ben, and Ben smiled, saying, "S-sure. Sure we are. Aren't we?"

Sherry said, "Oh yeah, we sure are. Whatever you say, Mr. Carter." She didn't actually feel that way, but that is what she said.

"Good!" said the green-faced Mr. Carter, putting his weird, green, huge-veined hands together in front of him and smiling a horrible smile. He turned and said, "Follow me then, Children of the Night! Follow me!"

And the orange rubber spider on his shoulder suddenly rose up on a string and disappeared, as he went and rambled around in the darkness. They could hear him rustling as they took a few cautious steps forward, and then they heard what sounded like a heavy, rusty old switch being thrown.

The sound of electricity sparking echoed in the room for a moment, and then the lights (as dim as they were) suddenly came on. It revealed an astonishing sight!

It was a display right out of an old-time carnival freak show. Except most of it was safely behind glass. Ben felt his eyes goggle. In the background, coming through the hidden speakers in the walls, he could hear old-fashioned carnival music playing.

On the walls, huge, moth-eaten banners advertised wonders and oddities like a two-headed baby, a strong man, a bearded lady, an alligator man, and Musto the Mentalist, Master of The Magnificent Mind. They were all brightly-painted, garish old things, and Ben was really impressed by them. They were definitely all original sideshow canvasses. You could *smell* how old they were.

On the wall, between the glass display cases and the sideshow banners, were ancient pictures of midgets, sword-swallowers and fire-eaters, clowns, acrobats, people with no legs who walked on their hands, Siamese twins, men with werewolf hair all over their faces…and even stranger things. All the pictures were old black and white pictures, and there seemed to be a thousand of them. Ben knew he could never hope to take them all in with one visit.

And then there were the display cases. There weren't many of them, but, boy, Ben thought, they sure were a lot more impressive than the stuff they had seen so far. In one, wires on a red velvet cushion propped up a tiny human skeleton. At the feet of the skeleton was a card with the words: "Pygmy skeleton. Borneo. 1893."

"Wow!" intoned Ben.

"Gross!" said Sherry, and Ben turned around. She was not examining the pygmy skeleton (which Ben was secretly wondering whether was really what the card claimed), but was instead looking at an ancient bottle of yellow liquid that seemed to have something floating in it. Ben walked over to her, and knelt down a little to get a closer look.

It seemed to be a dead cat. But man, it must have been floating in that jar for a hundred years. Plus…there seemed to be something wrong with it. Ben looked at the little card on the table where the jar was displayed.

It said: "Two-Headed Cat. Indiana. 1902."

Suddenly, the weird, spooky tones of Carter rang out in the darkness. They jumped. They had been so impressed by the displays they had nearly forgotten about him.

"Actually the card is wrong. Dead wrong. As you can see, if you look closely enough, it isn't a two-headed cat. Not at all.

In fact, it's a cat that was born with one head, like every other cat. Except, unlike other cats, our little friend in the jar was born with *nine legs and two tails*. A regular 'spider-cat', if such a breed of cat can be said to have ever existed at all. Someone printed that card up long ago, and goofed. I've never had the heart to change it."

Ben looked closer. Suddenly, he saw all the legs of the cat curled beneath its body. And there were indeed a lot of them.

"It didn't live long," said Carter.

They walked past some more of the display cases. There were many strange things: a ship built in a bottle (which Ben thought was kind of boring), a display of old-fashioned torture instruments (which were all supposed to be "From the dungeons of Ye Olde Inquisition"), and a selection of rare insects displayed on an old board.

In one case, a spider was pinned to another cushion. The card beneath it read: "Deadly Egyptian Tarantula. One bite. 1924."

"Wow, look, this thing could kill with one bite!" Ben said, impressed.

They had followed the displays around, and Ben noted, a little sadly, that they had come to a door marked EXIT in dripping green neon. The rest of the display cases brimmed full with neat stuff like old aluminum trumpets that mediums supposedly used to talk to the dead, decks of playing cards used by famous magicians, a few weird knives and scalpels, and a length of rope that was used in some old murder 200 years ago.

Then there was the electric chair.

Sherry felt exhausted.

"Can we go now?" she asked, hope in her voice. He could tell she was ready to drag him kicking and screaming out the exit if need be.

"Yes dear," he said, a little sadly, while examining an old photo of a séance with a hugely fat medium. The medium had some kind of icky, gooey mess coming out of her mouth. In the middle of the mess was something that looked like a cardboard picture of a face.

"Ectoplasm," he reminded himself. The stuff mediums used to "materialize" ghosts was called "ectoplasm." But he thought it was probably just a fake effect. It still looked strange and gross.

Ben joined Sherry at the exit. There was something hanging near the door, a weird, orange thing that looked like it was made of painted wax. Ben thought it was just another dummy corpse, like the one they had seen coming down, and he noticed there was no card to go along with this artifact. He turned and found Carter standing right behind them.

"Hey, Mr. Carter, what's this?"

He turned and accidentally brushed against the hanging display. He sent it swinging by accident, and suddenly, they both heard a little crack and a plop. The arm of the orange dummy was hanging loosely by a few strands.

"Great idiot, you broke it! Geez, how much is that going to cost us?" Mary's voice was angry.

Ben looked scared for a moment, before Mr. Carter reappeared and said, "Oh, not to worry kids. That old thing has been hanging around for ages. Why, the slightest brush against it is enough to make it fall to pieces. I'll mend it when I get the time. Say, look here," and Mr. Carter reached up and pulled the arm off the rest of the way.

He held the end of the arm out to Ben and Sherry. They could clearly see the end of a human bone sticking out.

"I-it's real!" cried Ben. "It's a real, live mummy!"

Mr. Carter laughed. "Sure it is! And there's a heck of a story that goes along with it, too. You see, back in the days of the Old West, this particular gentleman was an outlaw, a bandit. He robbed stage coaches and had duels out in the middle of the street. Just like in the John Wayne movies. Well, by all accounts he was never very good at what he did, and eventually his luck ran out. He was shot down by the U.S. Marshalls while trying to rob a train. Bad way to end a life, I reckon.

"Anyway, he was as dead as a doornail, but his body was still fairly intact, so they took him to a local doctor who had a strange, new method of preserving dead bodies that was all his own. He made the luckless outlaw into a modern mummy, and then sold the body to a local showman, who toured the body around as part of his medicine show exhibition. Eventually, the body was sold again, this time to a carnival, where it spent many more years as popular attraction. Eventually, somehow, it ended up at our very own Flag Island Amusement Park, although it wasn't called that at the time. It was called Coleman's Amusement Park. Much better ring to it, I think, but that is beside the point.

"Well, someone had the bright idea to paint the old thing fluorescent orange, and put it in the 'dark ride' they use to have before they bought this place. You know, a dark ride is one of those spook houses they have where you sit in a little car and it takes you around to all the displays. Pretty cheap as far as thrills are concerned. Of course, this place is a vast improvement. I designed it and furnished it myself.

"Well, the story doesn't end there. Back In the Eighties, a TV crew came to Flag Island to film an episode of a popular action show. By that time, everyone had forgotten that this thing was real, and where it had came from, and the story behind it. They thought it was just another prop. Well, some actress was walking through the ride while it was closed down, preparing for a scene, when she brushed up against it…and the arm came off! Yes, that's right, this very one. Came off right in her hand. She took one look at the bone jutting out, and screamed her head off. The tabloids claim she was never quite right after that, but the studio tried to hush things up as much as possible. Fat lot of good it did them. Anyone at the time could have told you exactly what happened, although most folks today probably don't remember.

"Well, the script writer went back and did the research and uncovered the whole story of who this fellow we have hanging here actually was. Made for a great legend, dontcha think? Anyway, that's the whole sorry tale. A real humdinger, isn't it?"

Ben didn't know what to say, but Sherry said, "Well, we sure have had an interesting time here, Mr. Carter. Thank you for telling us that story, and we sure hope you can attach…that thing back in place. Anyway, I think we had better be going now."

Suddenly, a horrible growl erupted from the back, and they all heard something that sounded like the snapping of a chain, and the growls of an angry beast as it dragged the chain across the floor, slowly."

"Boris!" Mr. Carter yelled, and then turned, with a sincere look of panic on his face. He said, "I think you better go too! Hurry! He's hungry and having a little tantrum. You don't know what it's like dealing with him when he's like this!"

Suddenly, a shadow fell across the wall, and Ben and Sherry looked up to see a sight they would never again forget as long as they both lived. Mr. Carter hurried to a switchboard and pressed a button. A door quickly opened behind them, and Mr. Carter said, "Run, you fools! Run!"

They did.

They ran all the way across the amusement park, to the parking lot, got in their car, and drove home breathless, not stopping once to look behind them at the lights of the Ferris Wheel or the shadows of the Spook House.

17

The Body

Marge and Dino were taking a well-deserved vacation. They had never been to Las Vegas, and they were very excited about it. They had been planning it for months, and they were animated thinking of the fun they would have there. Of course, Marge was just thrilled to be going on any kind of vacation at all. Things had been rough in the electronics business lately, and neither of them had been on vacation in years.

So they packed up their luggage and headed out to the airport. Marge had never been on a flight before, and she was very scared. Dino wasn't bothered at all, though. He slept through most of the flight.

As soon as their flight landed, Dino rented a car and they took their luggage to the hotel. The food on the airplane had been pretty bad, so as soon as they landed, Dino and Marge found themselves a good restaurant. A real classy place with Tiki torches and flaming shish kabobs, and booths made up to look like little bamboo huts.

Dino ordered drinks and chips and they both had the best and most expensive meal they had probably ever eaten. Afterwards, Dino and Marge went back to their hotel room, where they noticed a strange smell. It was a sort of sickening, sweet odor, and Dino asked, "Marge, did you pack some food away in the suitcase or something. I think it's gone sour."

Marge said, "Dino, you know I'm smarter than that. No, I did not pack any food away in the suitcase. I wouldn't want our new clothes to stink, would I?"

They sprayed some air freshener, and then made plans for the evening. They first went out to see a show. Dino really liked ogling the dancing girls, which bothered Marge and made her slap him a couple of times on the arm. They left the show in a huff, and drove down the Vegas strip, taking in all the neon and flashing lights and still feeling a lot of excitement for being in the biggest, grandest city in all of America. At least, that's how Dino thought of it.

They stopped off at a nightclub, and watched a fat man in a white jumpsuit and aviator sunglasses sing Elvis songs. Of course, he finished his set with "Viva Las Vegas," but his version was so fast it sounded like the one the Dead Kennedys did on their first album. Marge was getting bored, so Dino said, "Hey, the night is still young. Why don't we go and hit the casinos?"

So they did just that. They entered, and right away Dino could spot the security thugs in their black sunglasses and fancy suits. *Made men*, he said to himself. *I grew up around those kinds of hoods in the old neighborhood. Bet everyone of them is a killer at heart.*

He knew better than to cross such men. He had learned that at a young age, when a friend of his, Vito, had tried to become a "made man" himself. He ended up running afoul of the local crime boss. Vito disappeared one night outside of his favorite restaurant.

They said he ended up "sleeping with the fishes," but no one was ever sure.

Dino put such thoughts out of his mind. Marge went and played the slots, and Dino went to the roulette table. His eyes lit up as he watched the little ball bounce around the wheel. A few hours later, and he was winning big!

Marge came over to him. She hadn't had any luck at the slot machines, but Dino was already a big winner tonight.

"Dino. Dino honey, I think it's time we got going."

"No way, Marge! I'm hot tonight, and when you're hot, you don't stop!"

Dino placed one more bet. This time, he lost most of his winnings. He crumpled, slapped his forehead, and said, "I see what you mean. Thankfully, I'm not out very much. You're right, Marge. Let's go. I am getting kind of tired."

They went out of the casino, through the lobby, past the autographed pictures of Dean Martin and Sammy Davis Jr., and Neil Diamond, and out to the parking lot, where a young man brought the rented car around for them.

He tipped the kid, and they got in, driving back to the hotel while Dino's eyes, as tired as they were, continued to drink in the sights and sounds and flashing lights of the big city.

Back at the hotel, they got into their nightclothes and tried to settle down. Marge had her hair up in curlers, and was busily reading a tourist guide to Las Vegas, and Dino was flipping channels on the television, looking for a cop show. Dino loved cop shows.

That smell was still in the room. And it was worse than ever.

"Gee whiz, don't they ever clean this place up?"

Dino made a disgusted face, and clicked the TV off. Marge said, "I know, I know. Don't it ever stink in here! I'll have to have a talk with the management tomorrow. I don't know how in the world we're going to be able to sleep! Where on earth do you think it could be coming from?"

"I don't know, but it sure is awful!" Dino pulled the covers over his chest as he settled down into his pillow, mumbling something about "you'd think at these prices they could do something about that smell."

Marge got up and started spraying air freshener again. She used up almost an entire bottle, and that just barely covered it. She got into bed, and had trouble getting to sleep because of the smell. It made her want to gag.

The next day they went out sightseeing, took in a museum or two, snapped a hundred photos, and went swimming, lounging by the pool. They had dinner in a Southwestern place, and Dino ordered the biggest steak on the menu. At first Marge (who was always worried about money), was going to object, but then she said to herself, *What the heck. He works hard all year round for it. Let him have his fun now.*

When they got back to the hotel room the smell was so overpowering that it almost bowled them over before they even opened the door. Dino yelled, "Okay, this is getting ridiculous. I

pay good money so we can stay here, and this is the kind of thing we have to put up with!"

Marge was holding her nose and choking.

"It's too terrible to stand. I'm gonna go down and talk to the management about getting us another room!"

"Yeah, go tell him we have to get another room, pronto! Hey," said Dino, noticing that the smell was worse the closer he got to the bed, "I think it's coming from here. Wait!"

He suddenly flipped the mattress off of their bed.

Marge looked down at the box springs.

Marge screamed.

Dino shouted and his eyes bugged.

They found what was making the smell.

The box springs had been hollowed out. In the hollow space, they saw a shriveled corpse, dressed in one of those fancy suits that hoods wear. The corpse was rotten and looked like it had been there a week or more. The smell was ghastly.

And they had slept right on top of it last night!

Later, Dino saw on the news that the corpse was believed to be that of John "Fancy Pants" Giovanni, a small-time hood that had a rap sheet a mile long and had disappeared mysteriously two weeks ago. He was believed to have made an enemy of a local crime boss named Irwin "The Parrot" Papageno. Apparently, some of The Parrot's boys had come calling on Fancy Pants, and whacked him. They then hid the body in the box springs of the hotel room bed, right before Marge and Dino checked in.

"Yep," said Dino, "he was a gangster, alright. Except he didn't end up 'sleeping with the fishes.' He ended up sleeping under our mattress!"

Marge slapped her forehead and suggested the next vacation they take should be to Hawaii.

18

Mary, Mary, Bloody Mary!

Lizzy had been invited to the slumber party, and she was oh, so excited. The older girls at school had never invited her over before to one of their slumber parties, and now it was almost as if she was one of them. She really felt good that she was finally going to be accepted by Becky Robinson and her gaggle of friends. They were all the most popular girls at school, and now she might be a very popular girl, too.

She packed up a few things, kissed her mom goodbye, and headed out to the car, where Becky was honking the horn. Becky's dad had bought her a brand new car for her Sweet 16 birthday present.

She got into the car, and Becky said, "What in the world was keeping you? I've been waiting out here, like, forever!"

"Sorry, Becky. I had to do some stuff for Mom first."

"Oh," said Becky, as if she could care less. Not for the first time did Lizzy wonder if she actually liked Becky or not. She knew that Becky was popular with all the most popular people, and maybe Lizzy just hoped some of that popularity would rub off on her. Becky could really be a snot when she wanted to be.

Of course, on the other hand, Becky could also be very nice. Like when she volunteered to help out at the hospital, or when Lizzy had lost her wallet on their class trip to the amusement park, and Becky had loaned her fifty dollars and then told her, "Don't worry about

paying it back, kiddo. I just wanted to make sure you didn't have a bad time."

So Becky had good points, too. Lizzy thought most everyone did.

They got to Becky's house, and already a few other cars were pulled up at the side of the street. Lizzy could never get over how big and beautiful Becky's house was, and how expensive the furnishings were. She almost felt like a bull in a China shop whenever she went inside.

The girls all assembled downstairs, and pretty much had the run of the place, as long as they promised to keep quiet. Becky's dad was going to be spending the evening slaving away in his office, and her mother told them, quite frankly, that she had a headache and would probably turn in early. That sounded great to the girls, who didn't want to have Becky's mom staring over their shoulders all night. That way, the figured, they could make popcorn, watch scary movies, sit in a circle upstairs, and talk about what boys they liked, who was cool, and who most definitely was not. It sounded like it was going to be a killer evening.

So they made popcorn, and raided the fridge, and they all went upstairs to watch a really gory, scary movie that Becky had rented special just for the occasion.

It was called *From Beyond*, and it was a real gross-out fest. There were mutations and monsters, and exploding heads and slimy things and it was all just a little too much for Lizzy, but Becky seemed to really like it. Even though, later, she admitted that the ending—where a woman scientist escapes a mental home to blow up a house where monsters are coming through some sort of doorway from another world—was really stupid. Like, where did she get a time bomb with dynamite perfectly made just in time for the ending of the movie? It made no sense. Plus, the special effects, as gross as they were, were, like, straight out of the Eighties or something.

Later, after they had eaten up all the popcorn, and were sitting in a circle talking about boys (Janice thought that Brent Johnson was "like the hottest boy in school," but the rest of them couldn't see it), Becky suddenly piped up with a suggestion.

"Hey, that was a really scary movie we watched tonight. Wasn't it?"

"Actually," said Lizzy, "I thought it was kind of dumb. It was really gross, though. I liked that part."

"Yeah," said Becky, a little thoughtfully. One of the girls chimed in, "Well, I sure thought it was scary. I bet I'll have nightmares. Oh my gosh. I don't know if I should tell you guys this, but sometimes I sleepwalk."

The other girls were silent a moment, and then Becky said, "Creepy. Have you ever hurt yourself while you were sleepwalking?"

"No," said the girl (whose name was Katie). "People who sleepwalk rarely ever actually hurt themselves while doing it. That's, like, a big misconception people have about sleepwalking, I know. But it's true. We usually end up okay. Just walk around when we're not awake."

"Weird," said one of the girls, reclining on her rolled-up sleeping bag.

"Hey, does anyone want to hear a really weird story?" asked Becky, with a sudden strange smile on her face. The other girls looked around a little nervously. After all, they were getting ready to go to sleep, and they didn't need any more weird stories or images filling their heads right before they rested them on their pillows.

"Depends. What sort of story is it?" asked one of the girls.

"A really scary one. You see, you're about to spend the night in a haunted house. Bet you didn't know that, did you?"

Suddenly, all of the girls grew a little quiet, until Lizzy piped up with, "Oh, stop it! You're full of it, Becky!"

Becky looked a little hurt, said, "No, it's true. We hear strange things all the time around here. Sounds like footsteps in the hallway, and then you go out to check, and no one is there. And then sometimes things get moved around, and sometimes it gets awfully cold in certain parts of the house, for no good reason. And there's no draft. We keep all the doors and windows locked securely during the cold weather seasons. And, sometimes, you can hear *moaning*…"

Becky trailed off, letting her voice grow quiet and mysterious, and a few of the girls giggled. Lizzy, however, felt a little nervous. She knew many of Becky's mischievous moods, and knew when she was just "pulling your leg." Tonight, she seemed pretty serious, pretty thoughtful.

"The worst thing is the crying you sometimes hear in the middle of the night. Sounds like a woman weeping. Guys, I swear, I'm not making this up!"

125

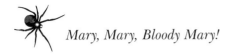

The other girls were quiet for a moment, and then a girl named Veronica said, "Hey, we believe you, okay! We just…didn't know we were going to be having our slumber party in a haunted house. Makes it kind of interesting, I guess…" Veronica sounded less than enthused.

"So, I guess now that you guys know, if any of you want to call your parents and split, now is the time, before it gets too late. Lizzy, what about you? You seem like the type that might be afraid of ghosts and things like that."

Lizzy thought for a moment, said, "No way. I don't believe in all that junk. And besides, if there is a ghost here, I think it is more interesting than anything else. I hope I get to see it. Or her. Or whatever it is. Is it a her or a him?"

Becky laughed, leaned back against her bed, and said, "It's definitely a her. And there's a story that goes along with that, too. You see that mirror in my bathroom?"

There was indeed a big, old-fashioned, ornate mirror in Becky's bathroom, in a frame carved from ancient wood in decorative designs of curly cues and other whatnots.

"Yeah," answered one of the girls, "I noticed it. It's a beautiful old antique, isn't it?"

"Sure is," answered Becky. "Except, the glass is brand new. Only the frame is the original. You see, the glass was smashed to bits a long time ago. We think back in the horse and buggy days. We think it was done by a woman named Mary. I used to ask her questions on the Ouija Board, except Dad made me get rid of it. Said he didn't like it in the house."

One girl suddenly piped up, "I've heard that if you burn them, you hear these terrible screams come out of the fire. I've also heard that if you try to throw them away, they always come back to you. I've heard that the only way you can get rid of a Ouija Board is to bury it."

Becky sighed.

"I think you've heard a lot of nonsense. Anyway. I threw mine out and it hasn't come calling lately. But the Ouija did tell me a lot of strange things."

"Like what?" asked Lizzy.

"Like Mary was this beautiful young girl who lived in this very house, a hundred years ago, And that she slowly went mad. She was obsessed with her beauty, and when she began to grow old, no one came to visit her anymore, and her boyfriend or whatever left her for another woman. Something like that. Anyway, she supposedly smashed the glass out of the old mirror in a fit of rage."

"Wow," said the girls, almost all at once.

"Oh, but there's more. Supposedly she used the pieces of glass to *gouge out her own eyes.* And then she used the pieces of broken glass to cut her face up so she was permanently scarred. I guess she almost bled to death, except a servant or someone found her and rescued her. They say she lived out the rest of her life a lonely, crazy old woman. And then she killed herself."

It was so quiet in the room, you could hear a pin drop. It also, suddenly, felt very cold.

The girls shivered, some of them clutching themselves. Lizzy asked, "How did she kill herself?"

Becky said, "Don't know. It never said. Just that she did, and now she haunts this house, weeping and wailing in the night. Oh, and there's one more thing. The Ouija said that, if you go into the bathroom in the dark, and say 'Mary, Mary, Bloody Mary' three times in front of the mirror, you're supposed to be able to see an image of her in the glass, all bloody with her eyes gouged out and her face cut up. I've never done it. Never had the courage. But, one of you might."

Lizzy, who had been certain so far that Becky was telling the truth, now thought she was just making it all up. Heck, that was an old legend. She'd heard it from a friend of a friend more than once, and she knew it was nothing more than hokum.

"That's…*stupid.* I'm sorry Becky, but that's just an old folktale to scare silly kids. Everyone knows that one. Heck, I can't tell you how many times I've heard that same story while I was out camping with my Girl Scout troop. You go into the bathroom in the dark and you chant the silly chant, and turn around three times, and she's supposed to appear. And sometimes she reaches out through the mirror, and scratches you on the cheek. Then you die mysteriously a short time later. Did I miss anything?"

The rest of the girls didn't know what to say. Becky was quiet for a moment, and then said, "Well, actually, you're supposed to go in there with a lit candle. Hey, I'm just telling you what I know, okay? It's up to you whether or not you believe it." She paused for a moment, and then said, "Hey, if you're so sure it's just a legend, why don't you test it out for yourself, huh? The bathroom door is right over there. Just take this candle," and Becky got up, went to her dresser, and got a candle in a glass holder, "and go in the bathroom with the lights off and try it yourself. Or are you chicken because, deep inside, you know I'm telling you the truth?"

Becky was all smiles, but Lizzy could tell that she was kind of steamed, just beneath the surface, so she said, "Alright. No biggie. Give me the candle. I'll go in the bathroom, say the magic chant, do the whole bit, and prove it's just a campfire tale."

"Be my guest," said Becky, still smiling.

The rest of the girls were unusually quiet, and not a few of them, Lizzy suspected, could actually feel their hearts begin to race in nervous fear. None of them said anything, though.

Becky lit the candle, and handed it to Lizzy, who turned around, carefully stepping around the girls sitting sprawled on their sleeping bags on the floor, and walked across the room to the bathroom. She glanced back, saw Becky smiling cruelly, and saw the rest of the girls looking at her with slightly nervous looks on their faces. She opened the bathroom door, and the light from the bedroom fell on the long mirror, just across from the old-fashioned washbasin with the old-fashioned hot and cold running taps. Suddenly, she felt a little nervous herself. The bathroom was awful big, and the shower curtain was closed. Was someone hiding in there, waiting to jump out and scare her?

She closed the bathroom door all the way. The candle lit the bathroom dimly, creepily, and she walked slowly in front of the mirror. She suddenly felt her heart thumping in her chest, but she tried to tell herself it was only her imagination getting the best of her. Outside, she could hear Becky and the girls giggling and talking to themselves nervously.

She put the candle down on the edge of the sink, and examined the mirror. Yes indeed, it was old-fashioned, and the carvings of the wooden frame were of a type she had never seen before. Very fancy, ornate, and obviously the work of some master craftsman who died long ago. She stared at herself in the mirror, not liking the gloomy light.

Suddenly, with a voice that was trembling a little she said, "Mary, Mary, Bloody Mary!" and then turned around three times. She waited. She was just about to turn, blow out the candle, and walk out of the bathroom when, suddenly, the candle began to burn low, and she felt a chilly draft blow in from nowhere. Her heart began to pound in her chest, and she looked deep into the mirror. She felt prickles of gooseflesh break out all over her skin.

Suddenly, the bathroom seemed to grow very dark as the candle burned low, and a red, hazy mist seemed to fill the mirror. It was like her own image was growing dim, and fading out, and something else was forming in its place. Lizzy stood there in terror and amazement.

There was an image in the mirror.

It was a head and shoulders, floating, in place of her own face.

It was a woman. Her eyes were gouged out, bleeding badly. Her face was streaked with huge cuts and running with blood.

Her mouth seemed to be trying to scream.

Lizzy felt something brush her cheek in the darkness. Suddenly, a horrible pain shot through her face.

Outside, the girls had assembled at the bathroom door, listening.

They suddenly heard a piercing scream. A real scream. It was no joke.

Becky pulled open the door, and Lizzy came tumbling out, weeping and screaming, holding her bleeding face in her hand and screaming that "She's real! She's real! Bloody Mary is real!"

Many of the other girls started yelling and shrieking too (except for Becky, who always remained calm no matter what), and suddenly Becky's mother appeared at the door, looking like she had been awakened from a dead sleep. On the stairs below, Becky could hear her father come pounding up the stairs, saying "What in heck is going on up there?"

Later, Lizzy would need thirteen stitches in her face. They had to call the paramedics, but by the time they arrived she had already passed out. Today, she says she can still see those gouged-out eyes and that bloody, butchered face staring back at her from the swirling darkness of the mirror, trying, silently, to scream from beyond the grave.

19

The Motorcyclist

Otto revved up his engine, sending up a cloud of dust and gravel, and ripped out of the parking lot of the Beat Café with a huge, angry roar of his supped-up engine. The day was gorgeous, and as the wind sliced through his long, greasy hair, he smiled to think what a strange, and scary figure he must be to so many normal people as they drove by him.

He was big and fat, and he always wore the same leather jacket with a skull and crossbones on the back. What's more, he always had a cool pair of aviator sunglasses on, leather pants that he could barely squeeze into leather gloves with studs on the knuckles, and a T-shirt from his favorite heavy metal band. His friends, now a bunch of old guys that sat around with their wives and kids on Sunday watching the games, always asked him when he was going to settle down.

He would just laugh quietly, tossing his head back a little and tell them, "Man, life on the open road is the only life for me! I'll be a biker until my dying day. I think I'd clean lose my head if I ever gave it up."

One of his friends, Sergeant Buff Henderson (who use to be a biker himself until he gave it up and joined the Army), would later remember Otto saying this, and sometimes it would get to him. And Sergeant Buff was not the sort of guy that let a lot of things bother or upset him.

Otto pulled out of the parking lot that day going way too fast, and so he slowed down a little, reminding himself that he

couldn't afford another traffic ticket. He had had enough of them before, and he didn't fancy paying them off one bit. Of course, one of the reasons he hated paying them off so much was that he was usually broke.

The wind rushed through his hair and bugs slammed into his clenched teeth, as he revved his hog up one busy street and down the other. The palm trees were swaying back and forth, there was a slight breeze, and he reached over suddenly, snapping on his radio and cranking it up as loud as it would go.

It was Tiny Tim. People use to laugh at him for listening to Tiny Tim. Then, they usually ended up regretting it later. Sock!

He usually didn't take any lip from anybody, and most people could tell that just by looking at him. He had had numerous run-ins with the cops, and had been in jail a few times. Big deal. You got as much respect as you were willing to fight for in this world, he figured.

Yep. He was one big, mean, two-fisted leather-wearing hard case alright. And he had a heck of a loud, noisy, rumbling, rip-roaring bike to match. The world was perfect, as far as he could see.

"Tiptoe, through the window, to the window, that's where I'll be..."

He started singing to himself. Then laughing like a maniac. Then singing again.

At that exact same moment, only a few blocks away Roscoe Barker slid his enormous butt off of a round bar stool at the Happy Times Diner, put out his cigarette, sipped his soda, belched, scratched his belly, and laid down a tip for the waitress. He smiled at her, pretty little thing that she was, and she smiled back.

She thought he was pretty gross, really, what with his tobacco stained teeth and gray hair and big fat gut. But it was her job to be polite. The afternoon lunch crowd had all but vanished completely, and the bus boy in the back was doing the best he could under a mountain of filthy dishes. It had been another busy day at Happy Times Diner.

Roscoe went through the glass doors, checked his watch, realized it was only 2:22 p.m., and that he had plenty of time still to get the shipment of sheet metal he was carrying to the factory. He had not been driving for the company for long, and he personally thought they were kind of screwy. They cut too many corners, and the guy that ran the place, Tim, was too young by half to be in charge of anything.

Or at least that was Roscoe's opinion.

He crunched on over to the bed of his truck. It was a standard flatbed, with a huge stack of thin metal sheets piled up and chained crossways to it. He put his hands on his hips, not for a moment liking the way this shipment was loaded. It looked dangerous, like maybe a few lengths of chain wouldn't quite be enough to keep one of those huge metal sheets from slipping off the back while he drove. He whistled to himself slowly, frowned, and then heard a voice behind him say, "It ain't safe, mister. That's all."

He turned around suddenly, a little worried it might be a traffic cop, and was relieved to see that it was only Crazy Eddie. Crazy Eddie was a strange little guy in ragged clothes that looked like they came straight out of a trash dumpster.

He was always walking around town, sweating and dirty and stinking to high heaven, and talking to people who weren't there. Usually people from some other planet. Or, so Crazy Eddie claimed. But he was harmless enough, even though he looked creepy with his ragged clothes and greasy, stuck-up hair, and wild eyes.

"Oh, hey Eddie. How ya doing, buddy?"

Eddie looked at Roscoe in that intense, strange way that made people try as best they could to avoid Crazy Eddie whenever possible, and put one hand on his waist, thrusting the other one out in a weird fluttering motion.

"It ain't safe. You can see that, *cantcha* Roscoe? It ain't safe to drive your truck with those metal sheets chained up

like that. One of 'em could come loose and cause a heck of a problem. You go out on the road like that, you're just asking for trouble."

Roscoe nodded his head slowly, frowning, and said, "Well, thanks for your concern, there, Eddie, but I don't really have much of a choice right now."

Eddie frowned, said, "Something bad is gonna happen. I can feel it."

And with that he turned, and crossed the parking lot, suddenly striking up a conversation with an invisible spaceman as he walked into the bright sunshine.

Roscoe felt a little uneasy, but he knew he had a job to do, so he opened the door of his cab, climbed in, and slammed it tightly, making sure to buckle his seatbelt (all he needed was to get another fine for not wearing his belt), and started up the monstrous, rumbling diesel engine, belching black smoke like a huge, fiery furnace on wheels. All of a sudden, he felt more comfortable. Yeah, this was the life. He hated being stuck inside a building like some miserable grunt, lifting and sweating while a gorgeous day like this just passed him by. At least as a truck driver, he got to get out on the open road. Vroom!

He peeled out of the parking lot, slowly, like a great iron elephant, with his chained-up cargo clanking and rattling in the back. He put an old battered cassette tape in the player. It was a tape of television theme songs.

Not far away, Gina Louise Sanchez was dropping off a busload of kids at their regular stop, thankful that the day was almost done. Behind her, the little monsters were roaring, flipping spit wads, throwing paper wads, paper airplanes, yelling and carrying-on, and acting like a busload of animals. She groaned, was glad to see the little monsters bottleneck at the door of the bus, and then go out into the sunshine of the neighborhood. It helped to know that the bus was getting cleared out, little by little.

She closed the door, shifted gears, and felt her mind zone out a little. Just a few more stops and she could get the bus back to the garage and get home. Then, she would unwind in the bath and listen to some relaxing music. She had downloaded some noise music from the Internet.

Otto was roaring down the street, had managed to pop two wheelies to impress a beautiful lady he saw walking in front of the shops, and then turned the corner, spitting bugs out of his teeth as he went. He weaved in and out of traffic, taking a few risks he knew he really shouldn't be taking, but unable to stop himself. He was feeling mighty fine.

Up ahead, Roscoe was shifting gears to make it up the hill. The old truck groaned and clattered and moaned, and the chains holding the metal sheets in place rattled and banged against the side of the truck as it wheezed its way up the hill. Behind him, he saw, some crazy biker was speeding up on his tail like a rocket.

The guy rode his tail for a little while, gunning his stupid bike as the road leveled out up ahead.

Otto was miffed; this big truck was getting in the way of his high speed joyride. He eased up a bit and made sure there was no one in the oncoming lane, and then revved it as fast as it could go.

Suddenly, the truck backfired and hit a bad spot in the road. Roscoe couldn't hear it, but one of the long lengths of chain holding the metal sheets in place snapped.

Otto rocketed toward the tail end of the truck, swerving around it just as the chain snapped, and one of the slick sheets of metal slid off the top of the stack.

It was like a giant razor headed straight for him. In just a split second of time, as Otto and the metal sheet came into contact, the biker saw his entire life flash before his eyes like a movie on fast-forward.

This particular movie was awfully short.

Roscoe looked out the driver side window as the bike came roaring past him. He was about to yell a curse at the stupid

biker when, all of a sudden, he felt his breath catch in his lungs. The biker roared right past his window. The only problem was he seemed to have left his head on the road behind him!

Roscoe felt his heart leap into his throat. Blood spattered his window, and all of a sudden a horrible pain shot through his chest. He was so shocked that the panic was giving him a heart attack!

His foot fell on the gas and the truck zoomed forward through the four-way stop. And, as luck would have it, a bright yellow school bus was coming through the intersection exactly as the truck came barreling through!

Gina Sanchez looked out of the driver's side window and saw the truck coming, but there was nothing she could do. Suddenly, it was like a giant sledge hammer socking the side of the bus. The kids still left on the bus let out a deafening chorus of screams; the bus went careening into traffic as tires squealed and metal crunched. People slammed on their breaks and jammed their horns and everything was total chaos!

Most people said it was a miracle, but none of the kids on the bus were seriously hurt, and Gina Sanchez made out okay too, although she had to spend several weeks in the hospital, as did other people. There were some people seriously injured in the wreck, but overall, it was not that bad.

Roscoe was not so lucky, though, His heart attack had been instantly fatal, and the paramedics could do nothing for him. His widow received a huge settlement from the company which Roscoe had been driving for when he died, and she was darn happy to have it. Word is she moved to Hawaii and spends her time on the beach listening to Martin Denny and drinking rum out of a wooden mug carved to look like a tiki head.

Otto (or what was left of him) was twisted into a gory pretzel mess on a grassy embankment not far from where the truck collided with the bus. Amazing, as the paramedics worked to unwind him from the twisted wreck, his radio was still blaring Tiny Tim. Tiny was singing that it was a long way to Tipperary.

Members of Otto's biker gang had a huge, smelly, noisy funeral procession for him, riding their hogs all the way to the graveyard, right behind the hearse. The funeral itself had been a weird mixture of bikers and some of Otto's more straight-laced friends.

One of them, a Baptist minister, delivered the eulogy. He said, "Brother Otto always said he would be a biker till the day he died. Well, I guess he got his wish."

As for Otto's head, someone told my sister's friend, who lives next door to the neighbor of someone who heard it from her hairdresser, that it was never found. Or, it was gobbled by alligators that live in the sewer. Or that Otto's ghost rides the night, looking for his missing head, and that people have seen a headless biker driving a silent motorcycle down the street. Or maybe it's the head that floats around looking for the body. I can't remember now.

20

Campfire Tales

Billy and the rest of his Boy Scout troop sat around with wooden spits in their hands, roasting marshmallows and hot dogs. Around them, the woods closed in as hoot owls and darkness were kept at bay by the crackling of the campfire. Billy slapped a hand across his neck and killed a particularly pesky mosquito.

They had taken a few hours to set up the tents, but it had been so much fun, and Billy realized he was never going to forget this special night. He had been unsure, at first, about joining the Scouts, mainly because dressing up in a silly uniform and learning to tie knots didn't seem like it would be very much fun. But once he got started, and then got his friends involved, it had turned into one adventure after another. He had to admit that he had had the time of his life this summer, and had made friends that he would treasure forever.

The fire crackled and sparked, and their Scoutmaster, Mr. Lloyd, said, "Man, those hot dogs sure do smell good, huh gang? I can't wait to dig in."

Billy couldn't agree more. He was so hungry he thought he could eat an entire package of hot dogs at one sitting. Plus, it sure was special to sit out here, under the stars, with some of the best guys in the world, and cook your food over an open flame. He thought that must have been the way the early pioneers did it, only they didn't have hot dogs, buns, and plastic yellow mustard bottles. They probably ate buffalo or something, but he wasn't sure.

It was no time before the kids pulled the hot dogs (which had become black and sort of charred but still tasted great for all that) off the ends of their sticks and had placed them on buns. They got busy handing around ketchup and mustard and sacks of chips and cans of soda from the cooler, and Billy thought that somewhere, out in the middle of space where Heaven was, his ancestors must, surely, be proud of how much he was roughing it out in the woods.

"Just like the Pioneers, huh gang?" said Mr. Lloyd, who was sitting cross-legged in front of his tent, and munching his hot dog with one hand while scooping baked beans off his paper plate with the other.

"Mr. Lloyd," asked Reggie Bannister, "what are we gonna do tomorrow? Hiking?"

Mr. Lloyd said, "I have a whole slew of special activities planned for tomorrow, guy. Don't worry about that. Tomorrow we work on 'trust-building' stuff. A bunch of different exercises and lessons. I think you guys will be really interested."

"Can we go swimming?" asked one boy.

"Can we explore caves?" asked another.

"Can we go hunting for Bigfoot?" asked another.

Everyone looked at this last boy strangely.

After they had eaten, and were laying back in the grass, their bellies full, someone mentioned that they should tell some scary stories.

"C'mon gang, I know you guys know some good ghost stories, right?"

The boys looked around at each other curiously. Surprisingly, none of them really knew of any that they could tell, right off the top of their head. One of the boys said, "Why don't you go first, Mr. Lloyd?"

Mr. Lloyd let out a belch, sat forward as if thinking about what might make a good tale to tell tonight, and then said, "Well, okay, here goes. This is an old one, but I heard it from my mother, who heard it from her aunt, who lived next door to a lady that this really happened to."

Campfire Tales

The Girl Who Lost Her Mother

Once, long ago, when the streets of Paris were still echoing with the hoof beats of horses and the rattle of old carriage wheels, a young girl and her mother came to visit the city as tourists. They were very excited, and when they checked into their hotel rooms, they could both barely contain themselves thinking of all the things they wanted to see and do. The girl said to her mother, "Mother, I want to go and visit the shops, and I'm sure you want to go and visit the museums. Let's split up, and then we can each see what we want to see, and then we will meet back here for supper. Is that not a fine idea?"

The mother agreed that, indeed, it was a fine idea. So they each unpacked their luggage, and, making sure to pick an hour when they would both meet up again at the hotel, they each headed out the door, barely stopping to wave goodbye as they went.

The young girl went and found a cabbie and went to the fashion district, where she went in and out of the shops, trying on this and that, but slightly disappointed that the prices of most things were much too high for her to purchase anything. She still had a good time trying on dresses and jackets and even wigs, and parading around in front of the full-length mirrors.

She spent many hours in front of those mirrors, imagining herself to be a rich, fashionable lady walking the streets of Paris in an expensive dress and being the envy of all the other young ladies her age. She tired of this daydreaming though, after awhile, and, leaving the area of the shops, went outside, and asked someone the time.

Oh my! she thought. It was getting late. She hadn't realized how much time she had spent in the shops, and she didn't want to be late in getting back to the hotel and meeting her mother for supper. So, hailing a cab, she went back to the hotel, went into the lobby, took the creaky old lift up to Room 342, and went inside, stopping for a moment to admire the rose-colored wallpaper and

142

plush, purple velvet hangings of the room. My, she felt as if they were staying in a palace!

"Mother? Mother? I'm here. We can go to supper now."

She walked into the room, and heard a groan. Moving into the shadows, she saw what looked to be a bundle of clothes on the floor. Her eyes adjusted to the gloom momentarily, and, with a feeling of horror, she suddenly realized that the bundle on the floor was her own mother!

"Oh mother!" she cried. "Whatever in the world is the matter?"

Her mother rolled over on her back and said, "Oh Dearie, I've taken ill suddenly. Please, help me to the bed!"

And so she did.

Her mother moaned and groaned, and finally said, "Oh, my stomach is hurting me something awful, dear! Could you not go and fetch a doctor to see to me? Why, I feel as if I might die right here in this bed!"

And so the girl ran out of the room and down to the desk, where she tried, with some difficulty, to get the desk clerk to understand that she wanted a doctor. He did not speak English, you see, and she spoke only a little French.

Finally, he seemed to understand, and, picking up a phone, dialed the operator. In a short time (that seemed like a very long time to the girl while she was standing at the desk waiting) a very old man with a top hat and a black bag appeared, and followed the girl back up to the room.

When they got there, he knelt down over the bed to examine her mother, who seemed to have passed out. He got up, and pronounced very gravely, "She is very ill. She requires medicine, but the medicine she requires is at my home, and it is clear across Paris from here. I will stay here and make sure she stays stable, and you must go to my home and fetch the medicine. Just ask my servants, here is my card."

And with that, he gave her his name and told her to go downstairs and ring for his personal driver. She hurried out of the room, to the desk, and did as she was instructed.

She finally saw the coach pull up out front, and hurried in. The driver seemed to know exactly where to go, but the streets

were so crowded, and the doctor's house apparently so far away, that it seemed to take forever to finally get there. All the time, she was worriedly biting her nails and feeling panicky about the fate of her poor mother, and wondering why she had taken mysteriously ill so suddenly. Whatever on earth could be wrong with her? she thought, nervously.

At last they pulled up to a stately-looking old manse on the outskirts of Paris, and she quickly hurried out of the coach and onto the porch, ringing the bell and waiting until the servant girl opened the door cautiously. She thrust the card and the note with the name of the medicine on it at the girl, and the servant girl seemed to understand immediately. She went back into the house, not inviting her in, rummaged around in some cabinets, and then appeared again holding a brown bottle. The servant girl then thrust the bottle into her hand, and closed the door without saying a word.

She walked from the porch quickly, got back into the coach, and said, "Driver, back to the hotel, quickly!" in her best French. She then settled back and waited, hoping everything would turn out okay in the end.

The coach ride seemed to take forever to get back to the hotel, and she noticed they seemed to be taking an entirely different route to get back than the route they had taken to get out to the old house in the first place. Somewhat angry, the girl leaned out of the carriage window and said, "Driver! Could you please hurry! I'm afraid it's a matter of life or death!"

The driver just seemed to ignore her, and the rest of the trip seemed to take just as long.

Finally, as twilight was creeping up and casting long shadows across the Paris streets, the carriage rattled up in front of the hotel, and the girl jumped out, hurrying up the steps and through the fancy glass doors, and making her way to the creaky old lift to Room 342. She had trouble, for a brief, panicky moment, finding it, but finally found 342 in the dense, gloomy maze of doorways, and rushing in, she cried, "I've finally returned with the medicine, Doctor Naudet! I'm here!"

She then stopped. The room was dark. Her eyes scanned the room, adjusting to the light, but she could see, almost immediately, that something was very wrong.

To begin with, she wondered for a moment, if she was not in the wrong room. The wallpaper, which had been rose-colored and very bright, was now a dark, ugly shade of brown, and the purple velvet drapes had been replaced with green drapes that were very plain and ordinary-looking. She went back outside to check the number on the hotel room door. 342. This was the room, alright.

She went inside. There was no Doctor Naudet, and her mother was gone. What's more, the bed looked as if it hadn't been laid on all day. Perhaps they had finally taken her mother to the hospital? But then, how did that explain that the wallpaper was different, and the drapes? She didn't know. She could feel a real sense of horror begin to creep inside of her heart. It turned her stomach to butterflies.

Racing back to the lift, still holding the brown bottle, she went to the desk clerk, who was now, oddly, dressed in an entirely different set of clothes. She was sure it was the same young man, though.

"Could you please tell me what has happened to my mother?" she yelled. "My mother! My mother was very sick. She was with Doctor Naudet a few hours ago, and he sent me to get some medicine! Now they are both missing, and the room looks as if it has been completely changed! I don't understand at all! Could you please help me? Can anyone please help me to understand all this?"

And the girl started to go into a hysterical fit, but the desk clerk acted as if he didn't understand a thing she was talking about, or even remember who she was. He took out the desk registration and looked for her and her mother's names, but could find neither (or so he claimed) and decided that, since the girl was having a fit and causing a scene, he was going to have to call the police. Which he did.

The police arrived shortly, while the girl was still screaming her name and the name of Dr Naudet, and the name of her mother. She was still clutching the brown bottle. The policeman took the bottle from her, uncorked it, and took a whiff. He wrinkled his nose and corked it again quickly.

"Deadly arsenic. You tell us someone named 'Dr. Naudet' sent you after this stuff as…medicine, for your sick mother?"

"Yes! He was right here in this lobby just a few hours ago, I tell you!"

"Do you have his card?"

"Oh, yes!"

The girl suddenly reached into her handbag to retrieve the little cardboard square with Dr. Naudet's name and address on it. To her horror though, she realized she no longer had it. She must have given it to Naudet's servant girl, who never gave it back. She whined, "Oh, the servant girl must have kept the card! I can take you right to the house, though! It's in a very fancy suburb of Paris! Oh, I'm telling you the truth! Why won't anyone believe me?"

She suddenly turned on the desk clerk.

"He's a liar! He knows what I'm telling you is the truth! He is the one who first called Dr. Naudet to help my poor mother! Officers, you should arrest that man! I suspect that this whole hotel is up to foul play, and is murdering the guests. That Dr. Naudet is probably in on it, too. If that is even his real name, and if he is really even a doctor!"

She broke down weeping, and the desk clerk merely shrugged his shoulders. The policemen looked at each other suspiciously for a moment, before telling the girl to, "Come with us, please miss."

She went with them, although at times they almost had to carry her out because she was weeping so fiercely. And where do you suppose they took her?

First, she was taken to jail, and thrown into a cell for insane prisoners. She was alone there, ranting and raving for her mother, and screaming about the "murderers" at the hotel, and about the "phony Dr. Naudet." The policemen had seldom encountered anything like her before. Finally, a judge ordered her to be put in an insane asylum, and there she spent many years, screaming at the top of her lungs in a padded cell, until, finally, when she was very old she was released.

She came back to America, changed her name, and began a new life. But she never saw her mother again, of course, and she never found out what had happened to her in Paris, so long ago.

"Aw, that was...lame." said one of the boys.

"Geez Mr. Lloyd, don't you know any real ghost stories?" asked Billy.

"Man, that was, like, hardly scary at all. Just....weird," said Reggie, who was busily toasting a marshmallow. He took the little blackened thing off of the stick and plopped it in his mouth, chewing thoughtfully.

Mr. Lloyd was a little disappointed, as he liked that particular story very much, but said, "Okay, gang. Anyone got any stories they think are better. Go ahead and tell 'em now, because it's getting late, and it's gonna be time to turn in soon.

Billy thought for a moment. Did he know any good ghost stories? That moron Deke Snyder had told him one not too long ago. Maybe he could remember it and tell it now. He said, "Sure, I got one, and it goes like this."

The Ghost Under the Bed

This really happened to a friend of my sister's boyfriend's next door neighbor. Anyway, he got this creepy email. It said something like:

> Warning! You must forward this email to at least five people! If you do not, the ghost of the woman pictured below will come and will kill you! This woman was killed by the man sleeping on top of the hospital bed in the photo. He was a drunk driver, and ran over the woman in the street. Someone took this photo, and saw the image of her ghost beneath his hospital bed. Later, he died mysteriously, and a note scrawled in his blood said that this email must be forwarded to at least five people, if you receive it in your inbox. Otherwise, the ghostly woman will come for you, as she is angry and out for revenge! So make sure and forward this letter to five people in your address book or, beware!

Anyway, it said something like that. So my sister's boyfriend's next door neighbor forwarded it on like he was supposed to, and of course nothing happened to him. But he knew someone that received the same email, and that person ignored it. Just deleted

it. And you guys know what? The person that deleted the email, and didn't forward it…died. Yep. They found that guy ripped to shreds by what looked like long fingernails. It's a true story, too. Just ask Deke Snyder. Man, I wish I had that photo to show you. It was so creepy: A guy laying sick in a hospital bed, and, right underneath, a ghost with long fingernails and a horrible, mangled face floating just above the floor. Gives me the willies!

"Gruesome…but cool!" said Mr. Lloyd. Most of the other kids were just silent, although a few of the said stuff like, "Man, I'm going to have a tough time sleeping tonight thinking about that ghost and the long fingernails and all."

Mr. Lloyd stretched and said, "Well gang, it seems like it's about that time. Time to turn in now. Got to be up early tomorrow, and get a jump on the day."

And Mr. Lloyd poured some water on the campfire, causing a tremendous hiss and a cloud of smoke to waft upward. The boys began to choke a little, but it still smelled good to them; like all the rustic beauty of the great wilderness where they were going to be camping the whole, long night.

Later, when the boys were all in their tents, and curled up in their sleeping bags, Billy and Reggie and a couple of the others took turns passing the flashlight around, holding it directly under their faces to make them look spooky. They each talked in a low, eerie voice, like the guys who narrate the shows about the supernatural on the Discovery Channel. Each told a silly little story, and Bobby thought most of them were pretty lame. Finally, it was Reggie's turn, and he took the flashlight, held it under his chain, and said, "Alright. This here is a story to end 'em all. You guys have never heard anything like this before."

The wind howled, lonely and afraid, through the branches outside.

"Bet we have," said one defiant boy.

"Betcha haven't. And quit trying to ruin my story, man. Or I'll kick your butt! Got it?"

With that, Reggie began.

Yes, We Have No Clown Statues

Marcy Parkinson was going over to the Greens to do some babysitting and earn some money. She was eager about it; she loved kids, and most parents thought she was just about the best babysitter that money could buy. It was a perfectly nice day in the neighborhood, too. The sky was a deep shade of blue, and the leaves were just beginning to fall off of the trees, and the weather was cooling down some. Soon, she knew, it would be Halloween time, and she would really have a blast babysitting then.

She got out of her car, made sure to lock the doors, and went up to the front porch. Such a beautiful house, she thought, and I guess it *was* pretty nice: Mr. Green was an insurance salesman, and the family must have lived pretty good. They had a two-car garage, a big lawn in front and back, and the house was always painted and done up to look real nice. You guys get me? These were rich people.

Anyway, Marcy knock-knocked on the door, and a few minutes later Mrs. Green came out and said, "We're just about ready to go. Both of the kids are upstairs playing, but they knew you were coming, and we shouldn't be gone for more than a few hours. Dinner is in the icebox. Make sure Timmy washes behind his ears, and little Sandra likes to have a storybook read to her before she goes to sleep. Warm milk helps her sleep, too. If you need anything, here is our cell number. Don't hesitate to give us a call. Okay? Good. Nice to meet you and all, Marcy. We've heard great things about you."

Mrs. Green then clack-clacked down the driveway as Mr. Green pulled the Bronco out of the garage. She got in, both of them waved, and then took off. Marcy closed the door, and breathed a sigh of relief. She actually didn't like meeting new people for the first time. She looked around the living room, her eyes adjusting to the sudden gloom.

Man, this place was out of sight! There were all kinds of antiques and curios and knick-knacks—stuff that looked real

expensive. She was almost scared to move around in here; scared she might accidentally break something. She went upstairs and introduced herself to the kids, which was fun for a few minutes, then left them to play. She walked down the hall, passing the Green's bedroom (which was as neat and orderly as everyplace else in the house) on the way, and something caught her eye. She hesitated for a moment, not knowing if it was polite to go poking around in folks' bedrooms, but she couldn't resist.

She walked into the gloomy bedroom slowly, looking in wonder at the thing she saw there. It was a life-size statue of a clown, all done up in a kind of ragged hobo clown outfit, with a red button nose, frizzy orange and blue hair, and weird make-up around the eyes. She thought the clown face was really creepy, and actually looked a little bit like a skull. She got up real close to it. She couldn't believe how life-like the thing looked. She wondered where in the world the Greens had gotten it. It really made her feel uneasy for some reason.

One of the arms was stretched out a little farther than the other. She thought that was weird, too.

She started to turn around, and then turned back toward the statue. Super weird, she thought. It was almost like the clown's eyes followed you around the room. She wondered if it might be some sort of life-sized doll with eyes designed to do that. She shuddered; the thing made her feel really creepy.

She turned and started to walk out of the bedroom, still listening to the children playing in the next room. Suddenly she stopped, and her heart started beating hard in her chest. Did she just hear breathing coming from that thing? She stopped to listen, her back still to the clown statue, and she thought she must have imagined it. She suddenly spun around, feeling really scared all of a sudden.

Wait.

Wasn't the arm of the clown just a little further out before? Had the thing moved, or something?

She looked at it for as long as she could stand to. It didn't budge or breathe. She started laughing to herself, put her hand on her thumping chest, and said, "Girl, you need to get a grip. That's just a silly old doll or something, couldn't hurt a fly. Man, you must be really cracking up."

She went downstairs, plopped on the couch, pulled out a package of bon-bons, and began to flip the channels. There were a few cool shows on she didn't want to miss. About a half hour later, she could still hear the kids upstairs, and she went to check on them.

As she climbed the stairs, she slowly stopped mid-way. It seemed like she could hear something besides the kids playing, something that sounded like cloth rustling around. And the breathing, again. She shuddered. Maybe this place was haunted.

She had seen a show like that on the History Channel. Maybe this house had ghosts.

She swallowed her fear, and went to check on the kids. One of them said, "Oh, hi Marcy. Mr. Clown's been keeping us company while you been downstairs watching the tube. He's so friendly. Comes in every once in awhile to check up on us, too."

Marcy laughed. These kids had such wild imaginations. Probably seen that creepy old thing a thousand times, and now they thought it was real. She told them she would be back in a little while, and went back downstairs, careful not to look at the half-opened bedroom door as she went...and the smiling, evil-looking clown statue.

She had a wild imagination too, it seemed.

She went back downstairs and watched another TV show. A few minutes later, she got a call on her cell phone. It was Mr. Green.

"Hi Marcy, this is Mr. Green. I was just checking up on you to make sure that everything was okay."

She smiled. The Greens were great parents, alright.

"Oh, everything is fine, Mr. Green, the kids are still upstairs playing, probably wearing themselves out. Hopefully. Nothing to worry about. I'll get them ready for bed, soon. By the way, I saw that big clown statue as I passed your bedroom. Pretty creepy Mr. Green. Where did you ever find something like that?"

Suddenly there was silence on the end of the line. She could hear Mrs. Green talking in the background.

"Clown statue?" said Mr. Green. "Marcy, we don't own any big clown statue."

Marcy was confused.

"You...don't own any...clown statue? I...I don't understand. The thing is right upstairs in your bedroom. I--"

Suddenly, Mr. Green cut in and said, "Marcy, I want you to listen to me very carefully. Yes, we don't own any clown statues. I'm hanging up now and dialing 911. You get the kids and get out of there now! Do you understand me? We're coming right home now!"

The call was suddenly ended. Marcy could feel her heart hammering in her chest. She looked at the staircase behind her, frozen with fear. Suddenly, she heard what sounded like heavy boots walking across the hall, and a maniacal laugh. The kids began to scream! She suddenly rocketed off the couch, knowing she had to do something to help the kids.

She flew up the stairs, her blood coursing through her veins, and ran down the hall to the children's room. She flung open the door, her eyes growing wide, and she screamed so loud she could be heard all the way down the block, as her eyes took in the most horrifying sight she had ever seen in her entire life...

"Wow," said one of the boys. "That was...intense."

"Man," agreed Billy, "that was great, Reg. You're gonna be the next Stephen King."

Reggie did a little sitting bow, and said, "Thank you, thank you."

One of the boys yawned. He was the only one that felt tired, but they all agreed they should try and get some sleep. So they curled into their sleeping bags, but many of them were too keyed up after Reggie's story to do much of anything but lay there shivering with their eyes open in the darkness.

Outside, Billy thought he could hear boots crunching in the grass. And a maniacal laugh somewhere in the wind.

21

The Hole to Hades!

Vladimir wrapped his parka around his shoulders and shivered in the howling breeze. It was deadly cold here, but he felt even colder inside. The discovery they had just made had made him feel really uneasy; he wasn't sure just how to shake off the creeping feeling of gloom that seemed to be settling over him. He stood there, watching his comrades go about the business of setting up the sound equipment that would allow them to listen in on the mysterious noises that had erupted from the hole, and realized they had made a great discovery.

The hole itself was believed to be the deepest anywhere in the world, and Vladimir suspected it might lead all the way down to the center of the earth. He wondered if that was even possible, but then he reminded himself that sometimes the strangest of things turned out to be true.

Possible or not, once he made this discovery known, he would be celebrated in all the newspapers and television programs worldwide. He was a Party member in good standing, and Comrade Andropov would surely present him with a special medal of commendation for his outstanding achievements in the field of science. Of course, it would prove once and for all the superiority of Soviet science and exploration over the decadent, Western variety.

The winds of Siberia blew ice into his bones as he crunched snow beneath his boots. He walked slowly back to where his

comrades were working feverishly at their machines and sound equipment. He said, "Comrade Medvedev, what have you discovered so far?"

Medvedev turned and looked at him with a strange, troubled look on his freezing face.

"Dr. Bezmenov, I'm not sure exactly what to make of it. We have managed to obtain some recordings from that hole…Maybe it is better if you just listen for yourself."

The two men walked past the crane apparatus which the workmen had used to open up the hole, and into the makeshift shelter where Alexei and Yuri were standing at an old wooden table. On the table was a single, reel-to-reel tape recorder. Both of the men looked up for a moment with worried glances as the other men entered.

"You will not believe your ears," said Yuri. "We sent that microphone down as far as the cable would allow. Miles and miles. I tell you, it is the strangest thing I have ever heard."

"Yes," agreed Alexei. "Strange, and terrible. Really frightening stuff."

Vladimir smiled in confusion, and then spat, a little testily, "Well, play the thing for me to hear, and let me decide for myself. Okay?"

"Certainly," said Yuri, pushing down the button on the audio player and turning up the metal volume control.

Suddenly, the small shelter began to fill with eerie sounds. Moans, shrieks, wails of torment in many different languages. Some of the voices were Russian, and Vladimir could make out the voices of fellow Russians crying out in anguish for relief.

"Hey, what is this, some sort of joke? I don't have time for this nonsense!" Vladimir spat angrily.

Yuri looked at him with surprise.

"No, no joke. Those strange echoes and vibrations our instruments picked up, this is what is causing them. Apparently, there are many millions of people trapped below the earth."

Vladimir felt his mouth fall open but continued to listen. He made a frustrated motion with his hand, saying, "Turn it up! Up!"

Alexei did. In the background, Vladimir could hear what sounded like strange machines and weird hammering. Sometimes, the cranking and clanking of the machines was met by a chorus of screams and moans.

Vladimir didn't know what to think. He couldn't believe his ears.

"It sounds like something from a decadent American horror film!"

He listened some more.

"No! No, it's impossible! Impossible, I tell you."

"Yes," said Medvedev. "Yet, you can clearly hear it for yourself."

Suddenly, Vladimir stormed out of the shelter into the gloomy cold, the howling wind cutting into his skin like a knife. He stormed over to the edge of the giant hole in the earth, and bent low, making sure to hang onto the crane that the lowered microphone was attached to, for safety's sake. He listened intently. He could still hear the faint whispers and echoes and feel the odd vibrations coming up from the hole like whispers of smoke. He looked down into that endless, deep black, and suddenly found that he was afraid.

He stood, went over to the outdoor recording equipment set up a few paces away, and asked the technician if they were still recording.

The young fellow looked up anxiously, took off his headphones, and said, "Yes."

"Well, in the name of V.I. Lenin, let's hear what you are recording!"

The young man flicked a switch and turned up a knob. Suddenly, the strange sounds could be heard all over the encampment: moans, screeches, agonized wails, cries for mercy, and the strange sounds of chopping, hammering, stretching, pulling, and other, even stranger sounds.

Also, Vladimir could hear something in the background of the recording now that sounded very familiar to him. It was a huge roaring sound, with a crackling edge to it.

He realized it sounded like a great bonfire.

"Help me! The pain! The pain! Mercy! Mercy!"

A particularly loud cry rang out from the speakers. It was in Russian. Another voice cried out in what Vladimir took to be Chinese. Still another voice sounded like a decadent American being tormented with pain.

155

Vladimir had no idea what he was going to write on his official report. But he did not sleep well that night. He tossed and turned in his bunk, and he had strange, horrible nightmares.

In his dream, he saw an enormous cavern, with pools of fire and deep black pits crammed with suffering people. There were horrible torture devices and tools everywhere: the rack, the boot, thumbscrews, glowing picks, and huge vats of murky, filthy water with boards attached to them. On the boards were fastened chairs, and on the chairs, helpless people were dunked over and over again into the filthy tubs.

People went about all hacked up, missing eyes and limbs, and some of them were on fire. Everything was dark and miserable and filthy, and everyone was being tortured on these strange, medieval instruments of pain.

Suddenly, a huge blast of flame would shoot up from the floor of the cavern, and Vladimir could see clearly who was doing all the torturing to the millions of innocent people who wandered around like zombies, screaming in terror and moaning in agony.

It was too terrible to contemplate. He felt fear grip his heart.

They were grotesque, twisted little gargoyles, colored black, and red, and green, and some of them had horns, and bat-like wings, and all of them had hides that looked like they came off the back of a deadly snake. Their eyes were evil and cat-like, and their mouths were filled with dripping fangs, and forked tongues, and their hands were twisted claws with long nails that looked as sharp as razors. Some of them wore boots, and some did not, and some wore black robes, and some did not, and some wore what looked to be like old-fashioned leather tunics. And some did not.

But they were all horrible looking, no matter how they were dressed.

And my how they laughed and cackled with glee at the suffering they caused the hordes of people shuffling around them!

Suddenly, Vladimir noticed one of them cranking an old, rusted metal bar. The bar was attached to a system of gears and

cogs that operated a long table. On the table, a poor man was being stretched slowly. The sound of the gears cranking and the stretching of the man's bones as they popped out of their sockets was horrible to listen to.

The little gargoyle took a break suddenly, wiped sweat from his scaly, bumpy forehead, and looked at Vladimir with a look of evil glee.

"Room for one more, Vladimir! Room for one more! All are welcome! All are welcome!"

The creature broke into a horrible laugh, and Vladimir suddenly found himself sitting up in his bunk, clutching the sheets with whitened knuckles, breathing hard. He thought he must have screamed upon awakening, but he looked over at his comrade in the next bunk, and he was still fast asleep.

No! It just wasn't possible. There was no such place of eternal torment! Couldn't be. It was all just the deranged fantasies of superstitious fools who hailed from countries not as enlightened as his own beloved Russia. Yet, there was no mistaking those evil sounds he had heard yesterday. And there was no doubt about where those sounds came from: deep within the hole in the earth that their team had discovered.

Vladimir suddenly realized, with a jolt of horror and loathing, that he had managed to discover the most incredible thing in the history of Soviet science: the Hole to Hades!

Vladimir filed his report to his superiors, but they didn't like it one bit. They ended up destroying the recordings, all the evidence of where the hole in Siberia had been located, and swearing everyone to secrecy. Or else.

Vladimir was ruled to be a "dangerous subversive" and sent to a mental institution. He was released after 1990, but he was never the same again.

Afterword

Well, that was a weird and wonderful collection, wasn't it kiddies? I do hope you enjoyed our little tour of terrors, and know that you are greedily awaiting more. Well, you'll just have to wait for the sequel!

By now you must be wondering which of our trauma tales were real, and which were merely rancid rumors spread by word of mouth. Well the answer is: "The Mummy" and "The Body in the Bed."

The story of the "The Mummy" is short and sweet. Once, several decades ago, a famous television crew from a famous television show was filming an episode on the grounds of an old amusement park. Well, when a few of the cast members were touring the funhouse, the happened upon a hanging mummy decoration. When one of them accidentally broke the arm they discovered…a human bone sticking out! It just happened to be the earthly remains of an outlaw named Elmer McCurdy, who was killed by sheriffs in 1911 during a train robbery. Well, it turned out that this was not the end of the line for Mr. McCurdy, who was embalmed and displayed by an undertaker, before becoming a popular exhibit in carnivals and amusement parks for decades.

Mr. McCurdy finally made his way to an amusement park where they were filming an episode of the old television show The Six Million Dollar Man. When cast members first saw Mr. McCurdy "hanging around" they at first thought he was nothing more than a prop. Later, a broken arm set them straight on that matter! Everyone had by that time forgotten just whose skeleton it was hanging in the fun house as a display, until some careful digging revealed the truth. The rest, as they say, is horrible history.

As for "The Body in the Bed," well, that story has happened more than once! There are actually a few incidents just like it, but we can't relate them all here, as it is getting late.

 *Afterword*

For more information , you can check out the great books of Dr. Jan Harold Brunvard, a folklorist who collects the scariest urban legends and publishes them in books like *Curses! Broiled Again!* and *The Big Book of Urban Legends*, which is done in comic book format. (But which is most definitely NOT for the young kiddies!)

Or, you can visit the excellent website Snopes, at www.snopes.com, which has a listing for every urban legend under the sun. Or so it seems.

As for me, my little frightened friends, I must bid you goodbye. Try not to get into too much trouble while I'm away. You never know who (or what) might be watching...

~ Tom Baker